FLIGHT FROM EIN SOF

. . .

W. E. GUTMAN

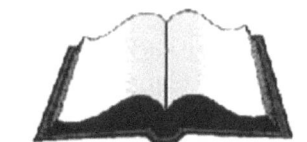

CCB Publishing
British Columbia, Canada

Flight from Ein Sof

Copyright ©2009 by W. E. Gutman
ISBN-13   978-1-926585-17-8
First Edition

Library and Archives Canada Cataloguing in Publication

Gutman, W. E., 1937-
Flight from Ein Sof / written by W. E. Gutman – 1ˢᵗ ed.
ISBN 978-1-926585-17-8
I. Title.
PS3607.U86 F65 2009   813.6   C2009-900633-2

Original art and cover design by Tony Cartisano, Norwalk, Connecticut.

This book is printed on acid-free paper.

Publisher: CCB Publishing
             British Columbia, Canada
             www.ccbpublishing.com

To a worker in the
vineyard of negentropy,
with heartfelt gratitude.

•

And to my wife, Linda
with love.

Also by W. E. Gutman

Journey to Xibalba –
The Subversion of Human Rights in Central America
© 2000, Reporter's Notebook (out of print)

NOCTURNES – Tales From The Dreamtime
© 2006, Fiction (ISBN 1-4259-5951-2)

ADRIFT – Life In Transit
© 2008, Autobiography (ISBN-13 978-0-9810246-9-1)

.. THIS TIME FOR SURE, THIS TIME FOREVER,
BUT IT TURNED TO SAND
SLIPPING THROUGH OUR HAND,
AS TIME SLIPPED AWAY ..
THE GRATEFUL DEAD

SCRIPTURE -- WHEN IT SAYS THAT
GOD IS ANGRY WITH SINNERS
AND THAT HE IS A JUDGE WHO TAKES
COGNIZANCE OF HUMAN ACTIONS,
PASSES SENTENCES ON THEM,
AND JUDGES THEM -- IS SPEAKING
HUMANLY AND IN A WAY
ADAPTED TO THE RECEIVED
OPINION OF THE MASSES.
ITS PURPOSE IS NOT TO TEACH PHILOSOPHY,
NOR TO RENDER MEN WISE,
BUT TO MAKE THEM OBEDIENT.
BARUCH SPINOZA

THERE IS NO ABSOLUTE, NO REASON,
NO GOD, NO SPIRIT AT WORK IN THE WORLD:
NOTHING BUT THE BRUTE
INSTINCTIVE WILL TO LIVE.
ARTHUR SCHOPENHAUER

IT IS USELESS TO TALK ABOUT REALITY
IN METAPHYSICAL TERMS AS REALITY
CAN'T POSSIBLY REFLECT THE FRAGMENTED
AND HALLUCINATORY NATURE
OF THE DREAMS THAT REALITY MIMICS.

UNLIKE REALITY,
A DREAM DOES NOT HAVE A "MEANING."
A DREAM IS ITS OWN MEANING.

PROLOGUE

A close friend, a fellow-journalist, inhabits his past the way Diogenes occupied his barrel -- a loner given to periodic fits of acrimony and despair.

Whereas Diogenes sought "Light" (knowledge) in the shadowy regions of human credulity, malice and stupidity, my friend retreats into the darkness of his own ruminations. Defying logic, given to self-treachery, he claims that everything that happened yesterday was wholesome and joyful. He dreads today. He lives in fear of tomorrow. A casualty of his own selective memory, he is visited by black-and-white recollections of a Gatsby-like adolescence, of doting parents and foppish peers stylishly attired in the latest art deco couture. He dredges up silver-screen memories of cruises to exotic locales, winters in Zermatt, lavish suppers at La Tour d'Argent in Paris, gala performances at London's Covent Garden and lazy afternoon tennis parties spent sipping Veuve Cliquot Champagne in fluted crystal glasses. He replays halcyon days filled with improbable metaphors further tarnished by the passage of time. He stopped wearing a watch for fear that each ticking second takes him closer to the brink.

In his closet, hangs the elegant ensemble in which he will be buried -- a black velvet Dior suit, a pink poplin shirt and an Italian silk vintage tie bought in Milan for the occasion twenty years ago. He fears death but, damn it, he will put himself on display in an open casket, suitably made up, a hint of rouge adorning his lips, a white carnation pinned to his lapel. He cares not a whit about life but he will take his final curtain call with studied chic.

"You don't find that bizarre," I ask. "Or paradoxical?"

"That's who I am," my friend pleads.

"That's who you engineered," I retort.

"I can't change."

"You refuse to change. Misery loves company."

The humble reed sways and bends and yields in the wind. The mighty oak tenses up and resists, snapping like a twig and toppling over. Everyone can change. I feel sorry for my friend but I've stopped preaching the virtues of positive thinking, will power and optimism. His is a hopeless case. Yesterday is an unforgiving prison. He has committed himself there until the end of time.

In stark contrast, I live on the cusp of a never-ending tomorrow. A lifetime of inauspicious yesterdays has taught me to steer clear of the past and to keep an eagle eye on the future. The past is gone. It can't be altered, revived or updated. I revisit it on occasion when memory beckons but the sojourn is brief and utterly lacking the tinges of maudlin melancholy that color my friend's reminiscences and poison his existence.

Unlike my friend, who is mired in the rose water-scented dreams where yesterday's evanescent specters congregate, I feel no nostalgia, no regret. I find his narcissistic fixation on "olden times" a noxious fad and a colossal waste of time. The past is irreversible. I file it away in some dark and dusty attic where I keep bric-a-brac and junk.

More rewarding than tomorrow -- which can't be foretold, postponed or prevented -- is a dimension rarely glimpsed by the fretful or the hyperactive. It is so fragile and magical and fleeting a realm that most of us traverse it without notice, conscious scrutiny or recollection. It's a spatial and temporal continuum better known as "here-and-now," whose assets are squandered with gluttonous frenzy by the unmindful and the emotionally comatose.

It was in Ein Sof, where I spent what seemed like the mere blink of an eye, that I navigated, after months of frenetic but meaningless exertions, the troubled waters of introspection. How soothing it was, once back among the living, to reconnect with my inner self, to surrender to life's alluring embrace. Yes, I retold myself as time stood still: More useful than the past, safer than the future, is an existential realm that is tangible and lucid, at once fleeting and ceaseless. It's the present, a place not bounded by geography, a circumstance unmarked by clocks. For those who have the courage to settle in its ineffable actuality, it's the only place to be. Anyone yearning to break free from the shackles of the past and the ambiguities of the future will always find a warm welcome in its bosom.

I know I didn't have to cross such galactic distances to apprehend the obvious. But serendipity is where you find it. As I came to, cleansed and brimming with a thousand spare tomorrows, I thought of my friend and others like him who, submerged under the weight of a thousand yesterdays, shackled by myth and superstition, can find no peace. Because they have ceased to dream, they have also ceased to be.

•

To be raises an interesting inference. As I transited in Ein Sof's misbegotten universe, a part of me kept asking: Am I dreaming, or am I being *dreamed* by someone dreaming he is me? The question, the province of ontology (the nature of existence) and epistemology (the nature of knowledge) is simply this: Where does dream end and reality begin? Are my ruminations the byproduct of a heightened state of consciousness or the undigested leftovers of surplus meditations? Is reality a dimension only an involved observer can traverse? Or am I an accidental onlooker fated to replay reality through my mind's eye? These and other questions not easily enunciated with words and pondered many times in silent thought -- as well as in my sleep -- have yet to yield suitable answers. As I would find out, a stopover in Ein Sof, however brief, exacts its own heavy price.

ONE

I arrived this morning after a brief and uneventful journey. I have scant recollection of this crossing. I may have suppressed it. I was eager to leave, disembark and settle in, and I paid little attention to the featureless landscape that unrolled before me. Unlike my travels of yore, when every ripple on the open sea, every cloud, every blade of grass, every flower picked along the way enthralled me, this voyage elicited only impatience. Not so very long ago I had dawdled, happy to suspend the moment as ports-of-call sang their siren song in the distance. Meandering to the antipodes and back had helped quell boredom, quench recurring pangs of wanderlust. I likened these expeditions to hitching a ride on a time machine that defies the sameness of immovable space: I sought in transience an antidote against immutability.

Wars, migrations and expatriations (or was it ruthless heredity?) had predisposed me to the meanderings that would highlight much of my life. Suitcases, always at the ready, were to me what wings are to birds, devices by which one takes flight, instruments of escape.

In a rare moment of controlled frustration, my mother had once astutely remarked, "When you're *here*, you're restless and melancholy, so you go *there*. And when you're *there*, you can't wait to move on. Where in this vast creation can you ever find contentment," she asked. I remember blurting out, unconsciously, what must have been a self-evident truth.

"In between, mama, in between."

Time moves on with unrelenting swiftness. With it comes change, some unforeseen, some unmanageable. "Time," said Henri Bergson, "is what hinders everything from being ceded all at once." His was an optimist's perspective. Time is a thief: it takes back everything it cedes -- itself included.

It was in haste and with a feeling of relief that I now proceeded toward my final destination. If you recall, it had been a year of gloomy forecasts and apocalyptic omens. Crops were dying, ravaged by torrential rains, droughts and cyclonic winds. Starvation was spreading across the globe and those who were not yet dying rioted in the streets and paid with their lives at the hands of crazed constabularies and vigilantes gone mad. Dark passions, political and religious, threatened to envenom societies already weakened by decaying economies, corporate greed and unregulated capitalism. Everyone, even the most sanguine, privately conceded that a menacing morrow lay ahead.

•

Despite my protestations, friends and relations had gathered to see me off, some armed with useless offerings, others so moved by my imminent departure as to shed a few ceremonial tears. The tears, I knew, would soon be stemmed. Life has a way of dimming surplus memories. You can always count on those most given to mawkish displays to recover from the deepest sorrow. Time heals everything. And life goes on.

My instructions had been clear: No crying, no lofty words, no banalities, no expressions of regret, no outpourings of maudlin sentimentality, no long-drawn sendoff, no flowers -- especially no flowers. I'd always hated goodbyes, not because *"parting is such sweet sorrow"* but because I had detected, even as a child, a troubling insincerity in the effusiveness of the farewell ritual. I'd seen too many congealed smiles of regret and tear-imbibed handkerchiefs; I'd heard too many words of staggering triviality when silence would have spoken volumes. I'd witnessed too many gestures that bordered on hysteria but broadcast no sadness to know that people are capable of Oscar-worthy performances.

"Hate to see you go."

"Take care."

"We'll miss you."

"Have a great trip."

"One more hug for good luck."

"Love ya. Don't forget to write."

Oh, shut the fuck up! They all did what people do when they sacrifice tact and discretion at the altar of convention and vulgarity. I endured these theatrics until I could endure no more. I thanked everyone for their solicitude and bid them adieu.

●

My parents were there to welcome me. They looked well rested and beaming, their ghastly urban complexion now healed by a radiant tan, the kind of otherworldly glow that people acquire after a few months of retirement in the sun. We spoke about this and that -- hurried and disjointed bits and pieces snatched out of the blue. Life. The weather. The economy. The greed of the governing elite. The imbecility of the governed. Aunt Ernestine's goiter. Little Adam's Bar Mitzvah. We would reprise it all in greater detail as we relaxed, just the three of us, late into the long night ahead.

I can't tell you what a thrill it was to be introduced to my maternal grandfather. He'd left Yesod the day I was born, never to return. I also met for the first time my paternal grandparents, both of whom had perished in Hitler's gas chambers. They seemed none the worse for their ordeal, just older and grayer than they appear in the sepia-tone family portrait, the neat taupe three-piece suit and fedora my grandfather wore and the graceful beige silk and lace attire my grandmother sported a bit faded, their former crispness dulled by time.

They in turn presented me to my paternal great-grandfather Fabian, the one who carried bitter memories of his childhood well into adulthood, "Fretful Fabian," who, sobbing, had told my father of the indignities he suffered at the hands of his own father, Abraham, and the sly and wanton young woman Abraham took for a wife a month after Fabian's mother died.

Abraham, a prayer shawl wrapped around his shoulders and a skullcap cockily perched on one side of his head, smiled at me reflexively, the way strangers part their lips in token civility when first introduced. We did not shake hands. With five generations separating us, the blood that flowed through his veins and mine, the blood of Abraham, Jacob and Isaac, of David and Solomon and, who knows, maybe even that of the Jew named Jesus, seemed stripped of all dynastic relevance. Relegated to mythical status, the reviled patriarch examined me from head to toe with a mixture of languid amusement and detachment. He might as well have been gawking at a monkey in a zoo. He followed me with his eyes but said not a word.

As I weaved through this genealogical conclave, I also became re-acquainted with a host of long-lost uncles and aunts and cousins, many I'd never met before, others with whom I'd socialized on very rare occasions before I left Yesod for the golden shores of Ein Sof. They too displayed cursory interest in my person, uttering token banalities easily acknowledged with a nod, a grin or one-syllable grunts. Thankfully, they spared me the tedium of small talk.

That evening, we all gathered around a large table festooned with plates of sliced stuffed derma and sizzling latkes, saucers brimming with gefilte fish, kishka and vine leaves filled with rice, large platters of fried *mamaliga* squares daubed with sour cream, and tureens overflowing with piping hot *cholent*, an indescribable but savory mishmash of potatoes, barley, beans, carrots, garlic, mushrooms and fried onions. We drank fermented cider, schnapps and plum brandy. And this being Purim, we also scoffed *hammentash*, bite-size raspberry, apricot, and prune tartlets shaped like the ears of the dastardly Persian vizier Haman, the appendages by which, according to legend, he was hanged to avenge his genocidal plot against the Jews.

Jews celebrate victory or flight from persecution by eating. They mourn catastrophe and death and expiate sin with a fast. Our history is filled with feasts, abstinence and famine. Every calamity is seen as divine retribution, God's payback for the debauchery and impiety of his people. No disaster, no torment, however inscrutable and cruel is deemed trivial because every event, every setback, every tragedy is the manifestation of Yahweh's will. Upheavals and grief and misery are tolerated, if not subconsciously longed-for, precisely because they herald purification and redemption and are encoded by God himself. God has decreed that Jews may not defy their own destiny by repudiating Moses' legacy without unleashing upon themselves the fires of hell. This is why Jews, to this day, live in a state of controlled anxiety, the Diaspora's assimilated ones subliminally, the new Canaanites with greater urgency.

"When will it ever end," asked my great-great-grandfather Abraham rhetorically, his eyes fixed heavenward, his right fist softly hammering the left side of his chest, unaware that his grandson, grandson's wife and several of their children had perished, that they were now mere statistics in the nihilistic calculus of the Final Solution. No one had had the heart to tell him. Or he had forgotten. This form of induced amnesia spares weak men the trauma of storing up too much knowledge which, everyone knows, can render them mad. People at the table looked quizzically at each other for a moment then continued to eat.

"Never," I replied, breaking a leaden silence. "We are the *Chosen People*." My father, who caught the bitter irony of my words, smiled and poured himself another jigger of brandy. My mother looked at me, a grown man, as she always had, like a hen admiring her newly hatched chick. It was a look that had caused me great embarrassment as a boy but in whose reassuring tenderness I now basked.

Flight from Ein Sof

TWO

I slept a deep and dreamless sleep and awoke late, the lingering scent of yesterdays' banquet still wafting in the air.

My parents and I had retreated to the den after dinner. We chatted long into the night, catching up on the sacred and the profane, the sublime and the ridiculous: politics; the economy; the staggering cost of war; family gossip; life then and now; my plans for the future.

I recounted how pre-election fever had been sweeping Yesod, how stupidity, chauvinism and intellectual torpor guided would-be voters, not acumen or sagacity, how yet another regional "conflict" was looming, this time too close for comfort and threatening to consume contiguous states. One by one, I remarked, major industrial nations, enfeebled by hyperinflation, soaring national debts, double-digit unemployment and social unrest, teetered on the brink of anarchy.

My parents, who had once shipped me halfway around the world so I could evade conscription and near-certain death in a bloody war, offered words of reassurance.

"Well, it's all behind you now," said my father. I could always count on him to look on the bright side, even in the gloomiest of times.

"Not to mention that Ein Sof is nothing like Yesod," added my mother.

Both had sighed, a wistful look etched on their loving faces.

"So, are you here to stay?" asked my mother, a trace of good-natured sarcasm lifting one quizzical eyebrow.

"Time will tell, mama, time will tell."

"Oh, leave him alone," chided my father. "He just got here."

"I've no plans to go anywhere for the moment," I interjected quickly, mindful not to create a situation. I can't swear I meant what I said.

●

The family compound was abuzz with activity. My mother was fixing breakfast. My father was scanning the Ein Sof Times. Ravel's *Le Tombeau de Couperin* played softly in the background. Uncle Lazar, the one who had relieved his mouser, Fékété, of his duties after a dozen years of faithful service and built it a cozy retirement crate, fed a black and white kitten. I remember when the eccentric Lazar gave a speech, praising Fékété for his tireless loyalty to feline duty and introducing him to his understudy, Orozlán. Orozlán, it turned out, played with his quarries and the mouse population that year exploded out of control. Fékété had to be called out of retirement until a more industrious killer could be finally put to work.

Lazar's wife, Helen, who had once offered me a child-sized shirt because her memory of me was that of a lad twenty years younger, boiled a bushel of apples in a big copper vat. Helen's apple marmalade was legend. As was her crude sense of humor. A gifted blasphemer equipped with a rich lexicon of profanities, Helen thought nothing of lifting her skirts, showing her behind and spewing a barrage of obscenities at anyone who disagreed with her oracular opinions.

Sam, my father's uncle, the one who denied visiting relatives so much as a glass of water but invited vagabonds to his dinner table, quarreled with his wife, the acrimonious Meema, over some minor peccadillo. The old couple, mismatched from the start, shared a lifetime of rancor and antagonism, Meema the casualty of latent schizophrenia, her husband Sam -- Schmiel to the family -- given to anti-social eccentricities that alienated all but the most tolerant kin. How the two managed to produce two sons was, for many years, the source of scabrous banter.

Those who did not know Meema admired what they perceived to be a kind of heroic stoicism in her rigidity. But her pinched lips, furtive glances and calculated irascibility betrayed meanness beyond pathology. My father, who would be neither fooled by the sham solemnity of her demeanor nor tolerant of her frequent outbursts, had once told me that "Meema" was a bitter, ill-tempered shrew even as a young woman.

"She alienated everyone she met and devoured her husband from the moment they tied the knot. No one could stand her. Efforts to dissuade Sam from marrying her fell on deaf ears. We've all been wondering what he could possibly have seen in this fire-breathing monster."

My father would express the same qualms when I married my first wife.

Wearing a pince-nez, a bushy mustache adorning his upper lip, my maternal grandfather, a noted poet, journalist, jurist and Teddy Roosevelt look-alike, cleaned his pistol, the very one he had used to kill the man who had challenged him to a duel. The duel, the culmination of months of invectives and counteroffensives dutifully reported in the press, earned my grandfather, who had never held a gun, let alone fired one, what many considered a slap on the wrist. Reluctantly prosecuted by a sympathetic magistrate -- his challenger was unpopular, a seasoned duelist and a marksman -- my grandfather was sentenced to six-months in jail. He spent less than thirty days in a comfortable room, next to the warden's office where he continued to write, entertained family and friends, and ate catered gourmet meals. The remainder of his sentence was reduced to time served and he was released on good behavior. In his day, as in this, men of means and distinction, however reprehensible their crime, rarely faced long prison terms.

I wouldn't have recognized Uncle Yanosh, one of my father's cousins, had I not spotted him peeling grapes with a pocket knife and picking bread crumbs from the table cloth with a wet finger -- mannerisms that, I now remembered, I had watched, transfixed, the way one stares at a tic, a protruding nose hair or an unzipped fly. Yanosh's features seemed frozen in a perpetual grimace, his upper lip curled menacingly, his nostrils flaring as if some foul odor inhabited his space, a scowl conveying both hostility and exasperation etched upon his face. Never far from his reach rose in a neat pile a stack of paper towels. Next to them was a tall glass of water which he fed with maniacal regularity from a carafe his wife was duty-bound to refill. An empty carafe elicited a litany of half-muttered expletives in her direction. Every ten minutes or so, he ripped a few sheets, crumpled them into a ball and dunked them in the glass. He then scrubbed the palm and back of his hands with a vehemence suggesting self-loathing. I called him Lady Macbeth. The skin on his hands had acquired the sickly whiteness and texture of boiled chicken. I imagined him as a boy, engaged in furious masturbation, and conjured scenes of maternal wrath for having "spilt his seed and polluted his hands in the presence of God." The man had a wretched temper. He invited these unkind fantasies and I found myself disliking him more than the obsessive-compulsive disorder from which he suffered.

Seated across Yanosh, Aunt Mary, cradling two antique dolls in her arms, hummed a wistful lullaby, the same lullaby she had sung every night as she put her baby girls to sleep.

"Schloof, schloof, sheine meidele...."

Her husband (and first cousin) Louis, the elder of two sons Shmiel and Meema had managed to produce, tinkered with a Rube Goldberg-like contraption designed, he claimed, to "stretch time." A veteran of New Guinea, the Philippines and Okinawa, Louis was intelligent but utterly lacking ambition. He had earned a living pressing ties in a sweatshop in New York's garment district. He and Mary produced two daughters -- one who was eight, the other, still incubating in her mother's belly when I first met them. Now in her fifties, my pretty, dreamy-eyed younger cousin had been diagnosed with schizophrenia when she was thirty or so. I called it "Meema's revenge."

Uncle Jan (everybody called him Néné Jan) smoked a Turkish cigarette from a short carved ivory holder, sending aromatic rings to the ceiling as he quoted from Baudelaire, Longfellow, Wilde and other poets. His wife, Tante Yetta, a once-pretty but vacuous woman who adored her husband, listened, her eyes closed, her mouth agape, in beatific amazement.

Abraham, staring in the void, his eyes still set heavenward in pious devotion, sought in mute prayer the atonement of sins that he knew could never be expunged. His son Fabian, reliving his life, wept in his hands as he had, years earlier on my father's shoulder.

I looked at Fabian, replaying his now legendary history in my head. Thirty days after his mother's death, having complied with tradition by engaging in histrionic displays of mourning, lamentations, breast-beatings and tearful one-way dialogues with God, his father Abraham remarried. His new spouse, a pretty, young woman he had been screwing when his wife wasn't looking, produced three children. Fabian was just a teen when he was apprenticed to a soap and candle factory many kilometers from town. When he came home for brief visits he would be fed leftovers and forced to sleep in the attic in the stifling heat of summer and on bitter winter nights. His stepmother made him do degrading chores and took pleasure in humiliating him in front of her own children.

"Like his Biblical namesake," Fabian kept repeating as he wept," my father Abraham gave in to his new wife's frivolity and malice. He never intervened. I was not cast out into the desert, like Ishmael; I was dumped in a barren field where love and tenderness did not grow. I was not offered in sacrifice to God; I was immolated at the altar of indifference."

●

Stirring from his prayers like a man awakening from a trance,

Abraham looked around the large communal room as if in search of a caring pair of eyes into which he could peer, perhaps a silenced voice he could rouse without fear of rejection. Finding me, hesitating at first, he asked, unaware of the incongruity of his question:

"Tell me about the weather back in the old country. Are poppies in bloom? Have the cicadas begun to chirp? Is the air filled with the sweet smell of lavender? Are young maidens dancing at the fair? Are they wearing new ribbons in their hair?"

Everyone froze as if immobilized by some invisible force. All eyes turned on me.

"I'm so sorry, Abraham," I replied, a vague feeling of pity tugging at my insides. "Powerful storms ripped across the Yesod valley shortly before I left, killing a woman and sparking tornado and flood warnings. Winds snapped off trees as if they were toothpicks. Twelve homes were badly damaged, and several roads became impassable. Mudslides added to the devastation. Something to do with 'global warming,' you know...."

Grief and disbelief smoldered in Abraham's eyes.

"But...."

I should have lied. I should have told him what he desperately needed to hear. It would have been a *mitzvah*, a good deed. Me and my big mouth.

"Enough," Meema screeched, pointing a menacing finger at me. "You're not to address Abraham. You hear? No one talks to Abraham. Not a word!"

"Why not?" A hundred pairs of scowling eyes turned on me. My father placed his arm around my shoulder, led me away and whispered, "let it go for now. I'll tell you later."

Abraham scanned the room, bitterness etched upon his craggy face. He stiffened, adjusted his prayer shawl, screwed the skullcap on his head and reentered the sacred realm as Rachmaninoff's *Elégie* played in the background. Abraham's supplications turned to lament. His eyes flooded with tears.

I felt like screaming.

THREE

You must be wondering what Ein Sof is like. It's too early to tell with any certainty. What I can say is that it's a place like no other I've ever known -- strange and vaporous, distant, shrouded in a torpid and soothing insensitivity toward anything that is *not* Ein Sof. And yet, it's also exasperatingly familiar, the embodiment of every cookie-cutter township I'd passed through on my way to ever-elusive Shangri-las.

This could be *Anytown, Anywhere*, the carbon copy of a thousand unremarkable clusters of human habitation thrown together pell-mell and without regard for growth and looming overpopulation. And like all booming outposts, it's a community so self-absorbed, so utterly indifferent to the rhythms and convulsions that mark the world beyond its gates, that it proclaims itself the center of the universe. Outwardly bucolic and easy-going, inwardly fettered by all the habits and attitudes the transplants brought with them, it's a realm given to ethnocentricity and religious tribalism. Its denizens are bonded -- or cleaved -- by common ancestry, language, culture and doctrine. Hardened by custom and repetitive ritual rather than encoded bigotry, their brand of elitism appears to be stripped of overt hostility. For the rest, it's live and let live. Ask the Perpetuals (as Ein Sof's citizens dub themselves with gargantuan snobbery) why they limit contact with those who are not of their own kind, and they'll tell you that they're protecting ancestral mores from outside influences. It's a feeble argument endlessly repeated and vehemently defended. These are the same people who assert that they can find the answers to all questions by asking as few questions as possible and who, while preaching virtue, claim that virtue cannot be taught. Like humans everywhere, they cultivate specious or illogical arguments to justify their own values while rejecting the equally dogmatic values of their neighbors and compatriots.

Protagoras would have been proud.

Regardless of their race or creed, Perpetuals put a premium on what they call unpretentious living -- plain attire, time-honored cuisine, modesty and temperate language. It would be useless heresy to suggest that what they consider simplicity, humility and temperance might appear to others as ostentation, duplicity and conceit. This perception, were they to acknowledge it, would be blunted by what they would argue is their austerity. Indeed, Perpetuals shun all but indispensable conveniences, among them the telephone. Their aversion for remote voice communications stems from their belief that this "infernal device," as they describe it, interferes with their quasi-monastic lifestyle, which depends in large part on a conscious separation from worlds and idio-syncrasies that are not their own. The telephone, they insist, brings the "outside" into the home; it intrudes on the privacy and sanctity of the family and interferes with social interaction by eliminating face-to-face, intimate discourse. Naturally, almost everyone has a telephone, suitably hidden from view in some secret alcove and used only in unspecified "extreme emergencies."

Perpetuals make no effort to convince their neighbors of their right not to be like them. If anything exists, they insist, it can be comprehended only by those who engender it. It's one way of rationalizing an isolationist existence.

Life, as it were, revolves around the family compound, centering on shared activities reminiscent of the failed communal settlements of the 1960s. Those who don't conform, can't be convinced to change their ways or transgress against a member of the clan are snubbed. Like Abraham, they live in a twilight zone of abridged human contact and enforced silence. They can speak out; but no one answers. Ever.

Key concepts that form the core of Ein Sof's collective ethos include the rejection of pride and arrogance; the cultivation of diffidence, serenity and poise, often interpreted as "submission" or "letting-be," but perhaps better understood as a reluctance to be considered presumptuous, narcissistic, or overly assertive. Perpetuals greatly value harmony (even if it takes discord to restore it) and adhere to a strict hierarchy. Defiance of established rules, behavior or language perceived to threaten the idyllic uniformity to which Perpetuals aspire, and violation of the pecking order are sternly censured.

The thing Perpetuals fear most is the danger that non-conformists, dissidents and critics pose to the established order. It was not without some reticence and chagrin that my parents, aware if not always supportive of my once eccentric lifestyle and the great polemics my writings had stirred, felt compelled to drive this point home.

"Perpetuals," my father explained, shrugging his shoulders, "place a high premium on maintaining the unity of the clan. Their ostensible eagerness to submit to codes that impede free will seems at odds with the blatant egoism, distrust and hostility so evident in their daily lives. You may want to take note of this dichotomy."

"Nor do codes prevent selfishness and vanity from rearing their ugly heads, even in far-flung places like Ein Sof," my mother added.

"Looks like the virtuous always take refuge in paradox," I ventured.

My father laughed. My mother beamed at the son she had spawned.

Not surprisingly, members of the neighboring clans, all of

whom also live in self-reliant autonomous enclaves and are bound by the same social strictures and domestic obligations, treat outsiders with distant civility. They acknowledge each other with frosty reserve; they rarely stop to converse. "Separate but equal" comes to mind.

Equality has never been a guarantor of justice.

•

It took me no time to realize that I was breathing the air of sorcery and fear. No, it wasn't medieval witchery but the subtler Satanism of homogenized ideas. If legend and tradition and rigid convictions shape the Perpetuals' thoughts, actions, notion of the cosmos, of God, of an afterlife, then they must also perforce be the cauldron in which simmer all their fears, prejudices and dormant hostilities.

While freedom of thought and speech are tolerated -- up to a point -- freedom of action through radical speech is not. You may utter what you honestly think is true, if you express yourself with a tact bordering on circumspection. Open dissent and rabble-rousing, especially the kind that ignite the imagination and stoke the intellect, are forbidden as they threaten the power base and tend to disrupt the structured unity of the governed. Freedom of conscience, in any literal sense is a luxury that the Perpetuals forfeited in favor of group cohesion and safe, soothing, intellectual inertia.

Their idea of the archetypal clan is that of a monolithic group of related individuals who submit to a system of commandments, decrees, unwritten rules and hazy taboos that generally inhibit the exercise of pure logic. They reject philosophy, which is guided by reason, in favor of faith, which is steered by prophecies, commands, injunctions and strict adherence to traditions lost in the fog of antiquity. It would be futile to suggest that, guided solely by tradition, men will inevitably be led astray. The mere concept of an ethos that rejects or bypasses tradition is unimaginable to them. Or so they claim.

The Perpetuals' attempt to regulate their affairs through

revelation and tradition has led to an odd social contract that discourages freedom of thought and bans concepts that in any way contradict their self-view, which they fiercely defend. In such a system men are not united by free association; they are led by a "higher authority" consisting of self-anointed shepherds and arbitrary credos to which they must profess unconditional allegiance. Such society cannot survive unless it faces the world outside its own with a mask of unyielding if refined belligerence, feeling threatened to its very core by rational thought, whose voice it doggedly tries to silence.

Flight from Ein Sof

FOUR

I stepped out of the family compound this morning, in need of fresh air and eager to reconnoiter this latest anchorage to which I had so hastily retreated.

Fabian's incessant weeping, touching at first, louder and more dramatic when assured of an audience, had by now become unbearable. I can put up with tears only for so long. Heartfelt at first, empathy turns to impatience, annoyance and resentment.

At the far end of the hallway, Meema and Shmiel were at it again, with Schmiel hiding behind a wall of silence and apathy and Meema icing over in catatonic rigidity in her rocking chair, her lips pinched, her eyes ablaze and darting with fury at anyone who crossed her path.

My grandfather was oiling the barrel of his revolver and buffing the muzzle with a chammy.

On the verandah, Lazar spoke to the kitten he had adopted as if to his own son.

"You can grow up to outshine old Fékété. It's up to you. Eat heartily. Follow your instincts. And one day, when you've caught your share of mice, you too can retire and nap to your heart's content."

Abraham, statuesque, transcendent, almost godlike in his gold-fringed prayer shawl and white lionesque mane, quoted from Samuel:

> *"But if ye will not obey the voice of the Lord, but rebel against the commandment of the Lord, then shall the hand of the Lord be against you, as it was against your fathers."*

Néné Jan, in rare form, a cigarette holder screwed between his teeth, recited a poem by Hungary's poet laureate, Sándor Petöfi, as Tante Yetta napped on the damask settee, her alabaster hands resting on her lace-garlanded bodice.

> *How many drops hath the ocean sea?*
> *Can you count the stars?*
> *On human heads how many hairs can there be?*
> *Or sins within human hearts?*

Néné Buby, Fanny's husband -- I was still a child when he emigrated -- played canasta with my mother. A jovial, burly man sporting a Chaplinesque mustache, he suffered from a mild form of Tourette's that triggered intermittent facial twitches followed by pig-like grunts. Hard as I tried, I'd never been able to suppress a burst of hilarity which the gallant Néné Buby forgave with equal doses of stoicism and benevolence.

Kibitzing, Aunt Lucy, a fake chignon adorning her nearly bald head, tapped the floor with her cane. Having reached the venerable age of ninety-four, she suffers from chronic flatulence and the sound of the cane striking the parquet floor, she believes, covers the machine-gun-like barrage of farts she emits every few minutes like clockwork. I remember when she merely used to clear her throat, or move her chair, a stratagem that my father never failed to lampoon.

"O.K. Lucy, the sound effects are quite convincing. But what are we to do about the fragrance?" Aunt Lucy always pretended not to hear my father's wisecracks and kept on clearing her throat.

Across the drawing room, Lucy's baby sister, my maternal grandmother, now, 90 and nearly blind, read *Amok*, by Stefan Zweig, one of her favorite authors, with the aid of a large magnifying glass. A woman of great beauty, charm and wit, my grandmother had always been an avid reader. She enjoyed history and great literature -- Toynbee, Gibbon, Josephus, Flaubert, Balzac, Hugo, Du Maurier, Vicki Baum. It was a shame to see her struggle as she shifted the magnifier from one spectacled eye to the other. A confirmed Atheist, she often quoted Vicki Baum:

"To be a Jew is a destiny."

She distilled from this epigram more than just an axiomatic truth. She lived long enough to see destiny at work.

•

"Don't say too much. Don't ask too many questions," my mother counseled as she accompanied me to the door. Several pairs of eyes followed me with suspicion. "Neither be a chatterbox nor a snoop. Mind your own business," she said, adjusting my upturned collar. Typically, such injunctions would have annoyed me, prompting me to demand an explanation and, contrarian that I am, to flout it. But coming from my mother, who had always encouraged free thought and intellectual curiosity, and helped give wings to some of my more harebrained schemes, the advice seemed as much out of character as it was out of place.

"And don't venture too far off. Not everyone and everything in Ein Sof is worth knowing," my mother added, her brow arching in a frown that telegraphed apprehension and pleaded for caution.

"What do you mean?"

She looked away. "Do what I ask, please."

"Explain yourself."

"Oh, It's the Dybbuks," she answered dejectedly, looking at the ground.

"The Dybbuks?"

"We call them that. Others give them different names. Stay away from Gehenna."

"*Dybbuks? Gehenna?*"

She placed a forefinger against my lips.

"Shhh. Just don't wander off too far. And be home by suppertime. I'm preparing your favorite dish."

"Escargots in butter, garlic and dill?"

"Don't be silly."

•

It is in this genteel, lily-white section of Ein Sof where old-moneyed gentry and vulgar nouveaux riches coexist in mutual disdain along tree-lined lanes and neatly manicured lawns that I got a good look at this pastoral sanctuary. Red tile roofs. White picket fences. Pastel-colored communal houses. Flower and vegetable gardens teeming with fragrant blossoms and succulent legumes. An ivied gazebo at the center of a verdant public square. Tidy, freshly paved lanes radiating from the main drag to the housing complexes in a star-shaped pattern. An air of everlasting spring wafting on an island of apparent serenity. And nary a soul to be seen anywhere, save an occasional, furtive, specter-like figure scurrying about in great haste, as if in fear of being seen or fleeing the scene of some impending disaster.

In spring, summer and fall, I am told, crews of Perpetuals get together early in the morning to landscape large tracts of gently sloping meadows, the obligatory golf course and the park at the center of which rises a bronze statue of Zeno, the father of Paradox. They mow grass, trim hedges, prune trees and plant annuals. In the dark pre-dawn hours of winter, they plow mountains of snow, sand icy driveways and alleyways. No one has actually seen them perform these patriotic travails. Most everyone assumes it's all done by civic-minded individuals in the dead of night. Others know better.

Getting lost in a place I hardly knew was not on the agenda that morning. Out of prudence more than inclination, I followed one of Ein Sof's secondary arteries, a long, straight roadway paved with cobblestones, flanked on each side by willows whose branches met midpoint above it to form a shady dome of green and extending, as far as I could tell, to the horizon line.

I kept walking, passing row after row of multiple-occupancy dwellings each set on a cul-de-sac on either side of the main road, some flying oversized flags, others proclaiming their religious affiliation with statuary and sacred icons, others yet professing their loyalty to God and country by warning intruders that their homes were fortified with all manner of automatic ordnance.

Rising in the distance, faint at first, clearer as I continued toward it, a massive billboard straddled the roadway. It read:

YOUR ARE LEAVING EIN SOF
AND ENTERING GEHENNA
PROCEED AT YOUR OWN PERIL

The road ended abruptly in a rubble of shattered rock and splintered cobbles a foot or so past the sign. Beyond it a yawning incline ended in a sheer drop. Extending from the base of a deep abyss, a steamy chasm stretched below as far as the eye could see.

Flight from Ein Sof

FIVE

Gehenna's unimaginable Stygian depths spilled open before me like a lanced boil. Spanning an arroyo through which flows, like pus, a malodorous rivulet of greenish-colored swill, an old bridge heavy with traffic and swarming with street vendors, separates a would-be purgatory from the pestilential netherworld below.

Reaching the base of the bridge was no easy task. I followed a dizzying spiral of steep ascents and lateral downward convolutions, first through a darkened arcade reeking of urine where a teenage couple copulated against a wall, then down a fetid stairwell where rats, oblivious to it all, fed from a pile of fast-food containers, and, finally, around ditches and embankments covered knee-high with rotting refuse.

Escher came to mind. Then Kafka. Then Hieronymus Bosch. And when I alit under the arch, perspiring and out of breath, I knew I had set foot on some spectral domain where outcasts and wastrels, the spurned and the unloved congregate like ghosts doomed to roam the void.

•

On the long and narrow ledge that hugs the foot of the bridge lives a family of seven, perhaps more. Rawboned, spidery, disheveled, prematurely old, a woman folds and refolds, sorts and rearranges a precious few possessions with a tedium induced by boredom or despair or madness. There's a pile of soiled rags for bedding, plastic bags to shield against the rain, a metal box to keep the tinder dry, a pot, scorched, misshapen and overrun with vermin, a disemboweled foam-rubber cushion to lean against on starry nights, a frayed straw hat, a sooty, half-burned candle, a rumpled picture of a blond, blue-eyed, pink-faced Christ smiling quizzically at the world. Tugging at a fleshless, sagging teat, an infant squirms and whimpers with frustration.

The woman bares a toothless grin. Sitting on his heels, a man -- her husband? -- is busy pounding back into shape an unyielding slab of iron with a wooden mallet. The metal will not give but he keeps on striking it time after time with an obstinacy that bears little fruit. There is no emotion on the man's waxen face, not a trace of impatience or anticipation or astonishment at the futility of his Sisyphean ordeal. Staring into space, visibly exhausted but unwilling to quit, he persists, lost in a hypnotic syncopation that marks the passage of time.

Below, perched on an earthen mound overgrown with weeds, two toddlers, both flaunting distended bellies and herniated navels, rummage for worms. Barefoot, naked, soiled, green slime oozing from their nostrils, oblivious to the horror that surrounds them, they shriek with delight with every worm they pry from the muck. A few feet away, a young girl squats and relieves herself. A youngster, perhaps her brother, barely older and small for his age, sleeps nearby, one arm folded over his eyes to block out the light, the other extended and limp. Clasped in his hand is a small can of cobbler's glue. He risks not waking up. Oblivion is a one-way trip. Sniffing glue is a dead-end occupation. Literally.

"Hey, you!" I call out. Startled, the boy stirs from a dark, dreamless slumber. His eyes don't open fully but he reflexively

tightens a childlike grip around the small can of glue. Turning on his side, compressing an emaciated body into a fetal position, then stretching, he makes contact with reality. I place a reassuring hand on his shoulder.

The boy staggers to a sitting position, rubs eyes thick with stupefaction and insensibility, and grants me a lifeless, clammy handshake. An odious smell of uncleanness fills the air, soon neutralized by the pungent odor of glue on his breath.

"Where am I? Who are you," I ask. The boy uncaps the can of toluene-based rubber cement, passes the opening over his nose and mouth, and inhales deeply, avidly. I look at him, detecting subtle signs of aphasia. Averting my eyes, the boy answers in mono-syllables, seeking to save face in ambiguity and equivocation. But such ruse could well denote the presence of a host of other latent syndromes, all resulting from the corrosive effects of inhalants on the cerebral cortex.

"Where am I? Who are you," I repeat. Attempting a smile, the boy scratches a lice-infested head, and draws another long snort of glue.

"Where are you?" The boy chuckles dejectedly "You're in my world of darkness, in the accursed valley, Ein Sof's garbage dump. Who *am I*," he echoes, his inflection tinted with grim solemnity and bitterness, his voice raspy and sepulchral. Sniffing glue devours sinuses and lungs. It causes horrible hallucinations. Irreversible brain damage and kidney failure are never far behind. Such fate seldom deters those who, like this boy, seem to fear life more than death.

The woman on the ledge unleashes a barrage of invectives at the boy. I have trouble understanding the words but her tone and gestures convey impatience, disgust. The boy dismisses her with a wave of the hand.

"Screw you, you're not my mother," he mutters, with more than a trace of envy and sadness. We shake hands again, this time in a complex ritual involving palm-smacking and finger-twisting. He takes leave, a longing smile on his lips, and ambles toward the water's edge where other kids are busy sniffing glue as the river's putrid current travels its lazy course.

"Who am I?" he yells out, this time in the interrogative. "You tell me, mister." He laughs a raucous laugh, more like a bark. "Yes, mister, you tell me. We have many names. Try Azazel, Dybbuk, Ghoul, Zombie. To many we are known simply as *the others*, the ones consigned to do your dirty work. Pick the name you like, we'll respond."

The woman plugs away at her senseless chores, one arm still cradling the infant at her breast. Unrelenting, headstrong or mad, her husband continues to strike wood against metal. I see no change in its configuration. Invincible, it taunts the would-be smith. But guided by some exquisite obsession, he persists.

Overhead, vultures glide in wide sweeping circles, surveying life, espying death, smelling it down below in the bottomless, sulfurous pits where the corpses of murdered street children are dumped. Many of the birds are now perched on roofs and tree limbs. Emboldened by some irresistible effluvia, a few make landfall. Waddling from side to side, wary and cunning, they will fight for the vilest scrap of offal in their path. The leathery flutter of their wings sends chills down my spine.

SIX

"You must be kidding," I exploded as my father informed me that custom calls for the latest arrival to assume the leadership of the clan.

"No. I'm afraid you'll soon be asked to do your part," my father said wryly.

"That's crazy. I've only been here, what, not even a wink. What does an anarchist like me know about management, supervision, control? I've never had the slightest desire to lead, to guide, to enforce, no more than I've ever suffered being led, governed or controlled."

"The post is largely titular, ceremonial."

"I detest titles and the powers they confer. I can't stand ceremony."

"I know, but your powers would be limited to your own freedom of conscience. Majority consensus would still prevail in all matters of authority and protocol."

"What you're saying is that I'd be free to think but denied freedom of expression."

"Something like that."

"I'm not interested. I've never followed anything or anyone and I'm unfit to lead. Surely the clan can appoint a more suitable candidate. Trust me, I won't be upset."

"No. Tradition is clear. You're our newest émigré. You must submit, with poise if not conviction. But look at it this way: Sooner or later, another expatriate will join us and you'll be replaced."

"But that could take eons."

"It's in the nature of eternity to suspend itself ever so briefly and to defer to happenstance. Someone could land on Ein Sof as early as tomorrow."

"Or the next day or the day after that or in a month or a year or in ten," I protested.

"Don't worry. Providence is not that generous."

•

The invitation to head the clan came from Yossi, my father's younger brother, an otherwise kind man and astute businessman who had owned and operated a children's shoe store back in Yesod. His son Amos, my handsome cousin, a talented cinematographer who had migrated to Ein Sof after losing a heroic battle against AIDS, had held the post, reluctantly, for almost a year.

"You'll honor us greatly by taking on this provisional assignment," said Yossi, speaking before a gathering of the clan in the large communal meeting room.

There they were, Lazar and his apprentice kitten, his wife Helen stirring the contents of a big copper pot with undiminished vigor, Yanosh deftly peeling his precious grapes, the towering Abraham engrossed in Scriptures, Fabian crying his eyes out, the peevish Meema and Schmiel, looking bored and cross, my maternal grandfather, fixated on the blemish marring his pistol, Néné Buby, grimacing and grunting with unremitting regularity, Lucy, farting and striking the floor with her cane, Amos, his angelic eyes lost in space where he could glimpse the gossamer likeness of his long-lost lover, and Néné Jan puffing away on his

Turkish ovals and ready, should he get the chance, to declaim a few choice verses to a rapt Tante Yetta.

My parents, models of discretion, stood several paces behind the throng, cautious not to let their unease show through the perfunctory pleasure they felt compelled to display at that moment. I knew that look. I'd seen it in their eyes on countless occasions as I embarked on adventures that filled them with pride and disquiet.

"I'm flattered, Yossi, flattered and touched by the sentiment behind your appeal," I said with sham gallantry. "I know how much this means to you all but I'm not your man. Find a more experienced proxy, someone more suited to the task, someone with the leadership qualities and zeal I lack."

"It's not that simple," Yossi retorted, attempting an assuaging smile. Tradition...."

I resisted the temptation to cry out, "Fuck tradition."

"Consider my past," I pleaded instead. Rewind my life. Dissect my leanings and idiosyncrasies. Reread, out loud, the words I uttered, the tracts I published. Ponder the consternation they caused. Are you forgetting that I was a source of shame to many of you back in Yesod? Didn't one of you suggest, as I reported on the gory deeds of Central American death squads, that I was meddling in other people's affairs?"

Meema squirmed. She pinched her razor-thin lips and they disappeared in a grimace of contempt.

"Didn't another among you call me an *agent provocateur* because I spoke out against military adventurism and torture?"

Yanosh fidgeted with his grapes.

"And didn't you, Yossi, once complain to my father that my inquests into government corruption, the bestiality of man and the nauseating sanctimony of the Jerusalem rabbis amount to treason?"

Yossi blinked.

"And when I reached fifty -- not quite old enough to lay down my weapons -- didn't my favorite uncle ask, *'Aren't you a bit too old to play paladins?'* Troubled by my forays into the belly of the beast where I hunted down vampires, hadn't he added with a hint of irony in his voice, *'don't you think you should let younger men carry the torch for a change?'* And didn't I reply that age alone couldn't stop me from dissecting the horrors I witnessed, to expose pretense and duplicity and sleaze in high places?"

Uncle Johnny, my maternal uncle who, spellbound, had listened to my appeal now evaded my gaze. A well-to-do criminal lawyer who had specialized in defending men he knew deserved to be hanged from the highest tree, had once urged me to pursue a legal career. My fiery high school compositions, precocious gifts of effrontery and rhetorical acrobatics had so impressed him that he secretly lobbied my parents to send me to law school. But Uncle Johnny's courtroom theatrics, the flourish of his body language, the ostentation of his blackjack arguments against often blameless plaintiffs, his very assertion that the worst scoundrel ever to walk the earth is entitled to due process had seemed incongruous at the time and given me all the ammunition I needed to dismiss his counsel and reject his profession. Years later he had amiably scolded me and claimed that mine was perhaps the only "important case" he'd ever lost.

I remember asking, "What sort of victory would you have wrested had I ignored my instincts, betrayed my conscience and yielded to pressure?" He smiled with avuncular pride and shook his head.

"Like I said. You'd have made one helluva trial lawyer."

•

I shut my eyes for a moment, reliving the sterling epoch that had once been mine. I had created a persona from a large collection of fictional characters and re-invented myself over the years: Part activist, part rabble-rouser, a nonconformist filled with compassion for the voiceless and the persecuted, the orphan and the widow's son, an anarchist revolted by bigotry and injustice, and, at the same time, a misanthrope overflowing with revulsion for the human race. It was a dichotomy I could neither explain nor reconcile. On one hand, I needed to find and expose the tiniest of stains in the purest driven snow. On the other, the pleasure I derived from such commerce far exceeded any possible urge to inform. I treated fact as a prop. It was the mood, the emotions, the color my stories conveyed, the anxiety or the outrage they were apt to elicit, that made me reach for a pen, not reverence for the Fourth Estate, nor a fondness for the reader whose fawning esteem or scathing attacks I ignored at first. My aim was to cause anxiety and discomfiture, to remind the forgetful and the smug that the Emperor is naked, to keep the son of a bitch stripped long enough for all to see him bare-assed and trembling, to sting and confound men blinded by their own self-induced myopia.

"How else do you awaken a dormant conscience..." I once fired back at an editor enraged by my denunciation of a cardinal who cavorted with barrel-chested colonels and generals and their buxom mistresses, yet turned his back on the gruesome human rights abuses that took place under his holy dominion, "... but by prying eyes open and dousing them with acid? If man does not peer into the heart of darkness," I pleaded, "will God?" The editor tore up my essay. This would not be the last affirmation that "freedom of the press" extends up to but not beyond the editor's desk and those who own the presses.

Hadn't I asked in an editorial timed to appear on the Day of Atonement, "Who is this 'maker' who inflicts (or tolerates) atrocities for 'the good that comes from them'? What cunning and irreducible absolute orchestrates without apparent aim or turns a blind eye to the paroxysms that convulse his realm? What 'intelligent designer' remains stone-silent while the sobs of his creation are never heard? What 'ineffable' entity is this, whose ear is inattentive and whose breast is unfaithful to the huddled masses that call on him and seek his succor? What cruel despot decrees that his subjects will speak and live by words not their own, that they will blindly obey the injunctions of his self-anointed envoys, tremble at their threats, mouth off supplications and jeremiads and recite guilt-ridden prayers of indebtedness and adoration, all repeated *ad nauseum*, day after day, to a God who never shows his face, never bares his heart, never sheds a tear, never says he's sorry, a God who grants life and, with it, the fear of death?"

I paid dearly for indulging my vice. I was fired, lost friends and suffered the disaffection of family. I was shunned, isolated, censured, even threatened. But I never kicked the habit and remained habituated, less for the fleeting high it produced than out of respect for all the unpopular causes I'd championed, some out of conviction, a few out of spite for those who did not share my egalitarian views, most in tribute to George Orwell's definition of freedom: *"the right to tell people what they don't want to hear."*

I'd also become fearful of losing the modest acclaim I had worked so hard to secure. Although it proved unlikely that my tracts could radically influence public opinion, I had by now a reputation to maintain and I could not afford to surrender the modest momentum I had gained. I was getting published. My byline, set in bold face, appeared under a cameo likeness of me. I had an audience and fresh enemies to rankle and strike back at. Safeguarding such ego-boosting assets would exact an effort all out of proportion with the ephemeral pleasure they produced. Instead of catering to my craft, I was now busy feeding an insatiable momentum of self-perpetuation-by-retaliation. No sooner had my broadsides created the desired effect -- shock, indignation or sheer horror at the medley of human miseries I chronicled -- than I'd fire off another salvo. Eventually, what had been a youthful fantasy, a Faustian pact, would shackle a once happy dilettante to a tiresome reflex. I kept going just to see how far it would get me. I never stopped.

In time, while I eagerly joined in the intellectual skirmishes of the day, my polemics evolved from tactical weapon into strategic objective: Excavate the truth, no matter what it takes to dredge from the mire where it hides or is often buried. I had become a saboteur and an apologist for the devil in whose company I learned at long last to shed what Maimonides called "senseless beliefs and degenerate customs" and to embrace the truth, lofty and hideous, enlightening and damning.

I was in my mid-fifties and involuntarily "retired" (anyone deemed "overqualified" understands the sting of forced jobless-ness) when I decided to turn an informal journal into a memoir, a life story replete with escapades, heartbreaks and disaster, in whose pages I could comment on the world as I saw it, immune from the editor's blue pencil or the ever-present threat of censorship. Satirical, politically incorrect in the extreme, devoid of simplistic rationalizations, what I compiled in more than five years of writing and rewriting grew into an accolade to gonzo journalism, a tribute to my parents, a personal testament of self-scrutiny devoid of pedantry or false modesty, and an indictment of every stinking manifestation of man's sadism, greed, gullibility and, most of all, stupidity, which I define as "the passion for fixed ideas."

No, this was not a burst of male menopausal narcissism, exhibitionism, catharsis or the vainglorious hope of a literary ticket to posterity. I was driven by a compelling need to tell all, often with brutal bluntness and self deprecation, to relate a personal story that spans four continents and seven decades, and to do so in brushstrokes that deliver an unvarnished canvas of the people, places and events -- reality stripped naked -- that marked my life. I minced no words. I spared no sensibilities. I took no prisoners.

My greatest victory, I believe, had been one of self-conquest. I reached emotional and spiritual independence by shedding absurd beliefs, relying on my inner reserves of intellectual power, banning the past from memory, living in the present with an eye sharply peeled toward the future, and ignoring situations or events over which I had no control. This might not be a "Dale Carnegie" story of success or a Horatio Alger rags-to-riches saga. I amassed no fortune, didn't become an industry mogul, a tycoon. I moved no mountains, nor did I ever aspire to do so. If we measure success in terms of wealth and material assets, I'm a miserable failure. If it means satisfaction with one's own achievements, peace of mind, the ability to accept one's limitations and the *chutzpah* to believe in one's elusive potential, then I've reached the pinnacle of success, all that without benefit of motivational gurus who enrich themselves by exploiting the greed and credulity of their audiences. Last, I was a struggling agnostic for most of my life. I had since come out of the closet and breathed the oxygenated air of emancipation by proclaiming my Atheism.

•

I looked at Yossi and studied the eagerness in the eyes of those assembled around him. I saw not a glimmer of fondness for me, or joy or festive anticipation. Instead, what their expressions conveyed was the lurid zeal of fanatics bent on solemnizing, by their presence, the sacramental reenactment of their faith and most fervid convictions. It's an expression I'd witnessed at ritual circumcisions, Bar-Mitzvahs, Eucharistic rites, baptisms, communions, prayer vigils, tribal scarifications, evangelical revivals and exorcisms, in the eyes of hopeless cripples in Lourdes, in the trancelike rocking of rapt Orthodox Jews praying at the Western Wall, in the serene stupor of Hindu mystics and in the awestruck faces of children being read a fairy tale. I sensed neither sympathy nor a grasp of the existential dilemma they were forcing me to face. The clan's expectations were as unrealistic as they were unjust. How do you honor tradition by forcing it on someone who rejects it?

At an age when the weight of years softens even the strongest convictions and consigns lofty causes to low-priority status, I realized that I was still full of piss and vinegar, that little had calmed the storm within and that, if pushed against a wall, I was ready for a fight.

SEVEN

"We all know who you are," said Yossi, "how you reason, what you've said and done. But this is family. If tradition is to be served, if harmony is to reign, we must allow some measure of flexibility and...."

"Abraham is family, yet...."

"Abraham hasn't changed."

"Neither have I. The freedoms that sustained me then sustain me now."

"Have no fear. You'll not be constrained. We'll grant you ample philosophical latitude. Of course, we hope you'll not misuse or abuse it by spreading it indiscriminately."

Yossi chuckled. I wasn't amused.

"You're full of shit. You're granting me the freedom to hang onto to my convictions only to impose undefined limits upon them? That's something I can't and won't comply with."

"We are heir to our past. Our memories define us. Our traditions sustain us. All we ask is that you not vilify them."

"The memories to which you cling have a way of distorting the past and encroaching on the present. You're all so intent on preserving these petrified memories that you devise new ones as a bulwark against change. Memories? Traditions? All you're doing is glorifying a dull, unhygienic, inconvenient, conformist, trite, unimaginative, regressive, self-righteous, stifling and antiquated past."

Yossi was livid but said nothing.

"Give him a few days to think it over," barked Meema. "He'll come to his senses sooner or later."

Néné Buby grimaced, squealed and seconded the motion.

"You have a week," Yossi decreed. "We're counting on you. Do not shame us by declining. Do not challenge prophecy. Let's not quarrel with God."

"You don't get it, do you? You haven't heard a word I've said: I'm like a top-loading washing machine: I agitate. That's how I was built. That's how I must function. I spoke honestly and offered cogent reasons why I should be disqualified. Instead, you're all blinded by ideology and bent on re-staging, like automatons, what you believe to be some unalterable cosmic drama. Sooner or later, my apostasy, my intractability will be met with more than impatience or bitterness. How long before one of you, pushed to the limit, responds by putting a bullet through my head?"

"A lot of good it'd do," Meema snickered in a low breath. "Besides, the boy has no conscience."

My grandfather stopped buffing the barrel of his gun and looked at the others.

•

What is a conscience? Does anyone really have a notion of it that matches what it truly represents? Or are we talking about that hasty impulse that pits reason against the current? I'm not saying that we ought to live without morals. Morals are indispensable, especially in the confines of a collective existence. Humans ask themselves and each other moral questions all the time, according to their temperaments, faculties and limitations. It's not a matter of alienating morality, of living on its fringes, but of living *beyond* it.

Morality predates man's codified mandates. To ponder a moral problem is to confess that one may not be innately virtuous and that therefore one must aspire to virtue in order to fill a need.

"Virtue does not render man happy," said Spinoza, "Happiness renders man virtuous."

You ask, "How does one become virtuous?" A better question is, "how does one become free?" I know the answer. And there are those out there who would lock me away for fear that I might blurt it out.

•

Pity the muckraker. His travail is dissonant, his art off-key, his output seldom more than the disfigured fragments of a straying spirit in search of its worldly self. He seeks neither comfort nor reward for disrobing reality. He only wants to fondle the moods and emotions he unearths as he strays along a maze strewn with pitfalls. It is the moods these metamorphoses convey, the dismay, the outrage they might possibly elicit, that makes him reach for a pen, not the urge to enlighten or entertain. He will ventilate the shadows, stir the most offensive exhalations, but he can promise no *Light*, impart no wisdom, deliver no eternal truth. He conforms to no particular communion. He's afflicted with an exquisite curse: He was baptized in ink. It is in the blackness of night, where ideas incubate, that ink runs swiftest and deepest of all. I know. I've been swept in its ebbs and flows, never sunk, willing to risk drowning again and again with each pen stroke. The voyage is fraught with perils; the course is uncharted. It is the very nature of such journeys that compels those who embark on their diaphanous wings to ask themselves, sooner or later, whether it was wise to leave hearth and home when the old armchair felt so good, when the winds of conformity sang alluringly upon the moonlit waters of the inlet, there before them. For they are apt to discover on arrival at some uncharted port-of-call, as I did when I reached Ein Sof, that there had been no compelling reason to make the trek in the first place. For when all is said and done, at the very conclusion of their aimless peregrination, weary and confused, they will wisely conclude, as I did, that some ideals are not meant to be aimed at, let alone exceeded.

EIGHT

I can't adequately measure the anger I felt toward those pigheaded dinosaurs, a kind of pointless rage that obnoxious little brats arouse in the saintliest of parents. You know me. I have no beef with God. We parted ways long ago. The "supernatural" and mysticism are realms in which I have set neither mind nor foot. I accept the proposition that some unquantifiable *energy* orchestrates the rhythms of evolution and unleashes the cataclysmic spasms that convulse the universe. But since I never found any evidence of a finicky and vengeful paranormal over-achiever, I tossed the subject in the trash bin of speculation, irrationality and blind faith. Nor has the presumed existence of a workaholic creator/judge/jury/executioner ever inspire in me the slightest urge to worship it.

I also resented the prophets Yossi and his minions kept quoting: Jeremiah, Isaiah, Ezekiel, Daniel, Habakkuk, and their disciples for endorsing and augmenting with their own terrifying hallucinations the wrath that the Almighty threatens to unleash -- should they err -- on his beloved people. And it is only insofar as the prophecies were legitimized by catastrophes, from Genesis to the Crusades, from the "Holy" Inquisition to Armenia, from the ovens of Auschwitz to the killing fields of Cambodia, Rwanda, Sudan and beyond, that historical events have assumed the kind of metaphysical sentimentality that keeps otherwise lucid human beings in a state of controlled terror.

Prophets? Antiquity's talking heads. Prognosticators, soothsayers, fortunetellers and mystic diviners who spoke in riddles and esoteric babble designed to inspire awe and fear in the hearts of the masses. They must all have been bombed out of their heads on hallucinogenic mushrooms, cannabis, hashish, coca leaves and toad secretions; Resistol shoe glue had not yet been invented. They suffered from acute megalomania, monomania, egomania and a terminal case of thanatomania: a consuming preoccupation with death. They would all have been diagnosed as certifiably insane had modern psychiatry been available to people cowed by superstition, trembling with fear, pickled in gooey mysticism and predisposed to treat all inexplicable natural phenomena as the mysterious manifestation of an enigmatic, invisible spirit.

As for the "tradition" that would have me take the reins of the clan, however briefly, I found it inequitable and demented. To vest the powers of family rule in one man is to weaken the independence of both the ruler and the ruled. The former, charged with enforcing traditions, lacks the incentive (or courage) to change them, while the latter is constrained by statutes and protocols that deserve to be rescinded, should they so much as violate legitimate individual rights -- but never are.

●

What emerges from the doctrinal struggles that cleave society is a frenzied tug-of-war between conflicting ideas. Essential truths are often trampled in the process. Everybody has "beliefs," opinions, pet views. Much of our mental constructs are erected on a vast scaffolding of dogmas, generally someone else's, often someone who precedes us by decades, centuries, if not millennia and whose canons we never question, however skewed, antiquated or unjust.

Keen on cramming dormant brain cells, we adopt these creeds and tenets, we cling to them, claiming they are the offspring of our own cogitations because they encourage us not to think, because they shield us from what we fear most -- reality -- because they keep us warm and cozy in our self-created doctrinal cocoons.

Back in my day, as I do now without compunction, I faced my reality and I bared it with conscious self-abandon every time I composed essays and commentaries, aware that candor and disquieting facts will trigger caustic ripostes and bitter condemnation.

The deconstructionist arguments advanced by the rabble to malign my columns may have sounded, at first blush, rhetorically alluring. But all they did in the process was to articulate other points of view, none of which could legitimately claim to echo some irrefutable truth. In free societies, however absurd, all opinions are charitably granted a status of equivalence.

What also transpires from some of my detractors' critiques -- Yossi's warning that I not exceed the limits of "philosophical freedom" comes to mind -- is the malignant suggestion that finding and telling the truth is tantamount to apostasy. Everybody read my words, one by one, but they all stumbled on the verities they conveyed.

I don't pretend to have all the answers. I dig for the truth, groping in the miasmic darkness of ignorance and fear. I ask questions, some troubling, some unendurable. What I uncover will never be to everyone's liking. Muckraking is not a popularity contest. I take no special pleasure in chronicling the ills of mankind, for in them I discover my own frailties and shortcomings.

Yes, there are more opinions than facts and yes, we are enamored of them. After all, opinions can blithely disregard, defy and, if need be, corrupt the truth. Tainted fruits of ignorance and self-delusion (or planted seeds of malice) opinions can also conveniently overlook faulty data or peddle arguments riddled with ideological monstrosities. Opinions shield us from the risks of personal experience.

In the mouths of demagogues, personal convictions assume dangerous dimensions: They are no longer what can be borne out by deduction or experience but what opinion-mongers themselves can pull off. Regurgitated by imbeciles, they are promptly espoused by other imbeciles.

Voicing an opinion, especially unsolicited, is an incorrigible human reflex. Every time we inhale a wisp of fact, we exhale a gust of inferences. Opinions have merit when they stimulate inquiry and rational dialogue, when they embody essential truths, when they are advanced with lucidity and when, having withstood the rigors of scrutiny, they harmonize with the facts they endeavor to interpret. Opinions are worthless when, by their ferocity or absurdity, they inhibit the coherent exchange of ideas or, worse, when they are contrived to manipulate or obscure the truth.

Advocates of extreme political and religious dogma, as are some of my most virulent foes, have been particularly adept at blurring the truth to advance their own agendas (or deflect the glare of incontrovertible fact). The greater their zeal in promoting their causes (or silencing their ideological opposites), the more tempting it becomes for them to suggest that freethinkers, iconoclasts and gadflies (the vast majority of honest journalists) are not merely wrong but are actually engaged in some sinister cabal designed to expose impious or discomfiting truths. In practice, this mindset leads to brainwashing, as witch-hunts ancient and modern have shown.

Only those willing to question the validity of "conventional wisdom" ever get closer to the truth. Fallacious reasoning, licit as it might be, is a greater enemy of truth than an outright lie. It is the prison in which we lock ourselves to feign a clear conscience. As someone once remarked, a clear conscience is usually the sign of a very bad memory. This willful myopia helps subvert good judgment and defile the truth.

Troublesome facts, computed by rational minds, are more useful than myths peddled by uninformed or self-righteous crusaders. When flock mentality is at play, as it was the other night in the communal hall, it is the myths, alas, that capture the imagination of the majority. Inflexible convictions render men blind, arrogant and, carried to the extreme, mad.

Flight from Ein Sof

NINE

"Why do you insist on making enemies," my father asked as we sat down to a game of chess. "Have you learned nothing from the hostility, and chagrin your views and pronouncements have caused?"

My father never indulged in idle criticism. His was an irrefutable statement of fact, one that echoed the inner struggles that marked his life. Born and raised in near-poverty by loving but simple, unschooled and unmotivated parents, he quickly concluded that an education was his passport to freedom, physical and intellectual. Ironically, an education delivered him into another form of slavery, one that would call for an even greater degree of devotion and compliance than the disciplines endured in his childhood's confining theocratic milieu. Proud, principled, mindful of his reputation, he would spend the rest of his life obeying the Hippocratic Oath. He was indeed an excellent physician. He would have been a brilliant astronomer, tailor or blacksmith if that's what he had aimed to be. An unwavering sense of duty would have imparted dignity and worth to any task he undertook. He would have worked long and hard to refine needed skills. He would have peered into the blackness of space until his eyes gave out; crafted the smartest apparel; forged the finest horseshoes until exhaustion had weakened his grip. But I know of no occupation that would have given him lasting satisfaction, let alone happiness. Medicine did not. The career that was to free him from the bonds of destitution would become a burden that he valiantly and scrupulously endured all of his life while lamenting the frailty and imperfection of the human body and deploring the maddening inexactitude of medical science. The emotional toll daily issues of life and death claimed on a restless man convinced of the futility of existence was incalculable.

"Humanity is an absurd happenstance and a calamity," he said in a rare moment of unguarded melancholy. "If Sisyphus weren't so busy rolling his rock up the hill he'd be laughing his head off at us. But he *is* us."

A lifetime of empathy toward others, repaid with indifference or unkindness, had found him exhausted, depleted. Caring too deeply, he had discovered, can bruise the heart and harden the soul. The "long shortcut to nowhere" had turned him inside out and left him empty and vulnerable.

Unlike one of his distant cousins, a noted prize-winning writer, my father never waxed mystical about his roots. He derived neither strength nor pride from them. Grief-stricken at the loss of his parents and siblings, stunned by the sheer barbarity of the Holocaust, he first toyed with the idea that Jews had been predestined to martyrdom. He quickly rejected that notion and concluded that suffering is universal and indiscriminate, and that it begins at birth for both man and beast. Although he would never think of himself as anything but a Jew, his Jewishness was circumstantial, utterly devoid of affectation and lacking the visceral transcendentalism, the truculence that accompanied the clan's faith.

"An ant doesn't wonder why it isn't a butterfly. I didn't ask myself why I'm a Jew. I still don't. It would be *un-Jewish* of me to ask such an absurd question. I am what I have created. My whole is larger than the sum total of my hereditary parts."

It was this repudiation of an irreversible fate, of a fixed and inevitable future, bolstered by his view of the world as a godless and irrational affair of ceaseless striving and affliction that led my father to shake the last congenital remnants of religiosity. He would also abjure the Kabbalah, in which he had dabbled throughout his life. Like his father before him, he had spent countless hours "meandering in stupefied fascination" along its cerebral minefields. At first, he had felt intellectually kindled but the leaps of comprehension, not to mention the leaps of faith the Kabbalah demands, had left him exhausted and confused. Ultimately, it was the Kabbalah's hyper-deterministic character that prompted my father to dismiss this, the most arcane of all Jewish philosophical systems as "a disquieting pastime for the idle, borderline monomaniacs or candidates for lunacy." The Kabbalah, he would conclude, not only trivializes human hopes, knowledge, dreams and the legitimacy of voluntary action or inaction, it effectively discourages rational and deliberate action of any kind. Any system that pledges to temper human perplexities and lead to enlightenment through occultism, he held, delivers false hope and leads to disillusionment.

"A real man does not submit meekly to his maker's caprices. A real man takes risks. He challenges the very odds that are stacked against him." In this bitter advice I recognized both a veiled rebuke of his own father, a theosophist who fought boredom and sought refuge from his own inadequacies in the Kabbalah's misty realm, and an admonition to his only son -- me -- to stand tall and yield to no one.

Late in life, overwhelmed by old age, which he described as "a heavy garment," and bewildered by the Kabbalah's abstruseness, repelled by "the effeminacy of mysticism," my father sought succor and guidance from the "undeviating honesty of realism."

In time, he would also turn away from God, describing "it" as "blinkered, ethnocentric and self-absorbed." He would continue to read the Bible, however, until the end of his life. Far from seeking comfort, he was looking to topple hallowed heroes and challenge cherished convictions by pointing to the contradictions, the lies, the betrayals, the greed, the violence, the cruelty, the depravity, the bestial godlessness of man, the insufferable inhumanity of God. Concluding that all human actions and "godly edicts" are motivated by abject self-interest, he would find in the ancient texts the ammunition he needed to launch vitriolic attacks against the very lore that had suffused his childhood, drawing instant and furious wrath from friends, colleagues and family.

Accused of heresy, my father would find further evidence of human vanity and intolerance in their attitude, a revelation that inevitably engendered fresh assaults and earned him further scorn and alienation.

A few days before he left Yesod for Ein Sof, reflecting on his own metamorphosis, no doubt troubled by mine, he counseled against reckless pursuits and glib conclusions.

"Seeking the truth is not a spectator sport. It must be done in private, in a *tête-à-tête* with one's own conscience, away from partisan influences and purged of all acquired preconceptions."

The truth he had referred to was several orders of magnitude removed from mine. I can only imagine how painful it must have been for him to watch the comforting warmth of imparted beliefs irrevocably replaced with the chilling emptiness of reason. In the end, hollowed out, he had sought asylum in a vacuum that could never be filled. I must find comfort in the notion that he may have been at odds with the world, as I am, but at peace with himself.

●

"Enemies are not *made*, Dad. You should know this better than anyone. Didn't you once exhort me to fight for what I believe? Enemies lie dormant, like a wicked virus ready to invade a vulnerable host. They exist, like nettles and poison oak and scorpions and asps. They thrive and proliferate like dandelions and crab grass. Favorable winds -- hatred, envy, greed, contempt, ignorance -- carry their seeds to the four corners. The odium with which my enemies are filled is a reflection of their personalities. A snake produces venom whether it intends to strike at a prey or not.

'Just in case' is the motto of the human predator."

My father sighed. "You're right but logic and reason, however clearly and rationally expounded, can't bring back 20/20 vision to those who suffer from self-inflicted myopia. You can't change reality, let alone alter the reality that others choose to acknowledge or ignore. Not here. Not in Ein Sof. What you see, what you hear, what you experience, tangibly and abstractly, is immovable, final."

As he spoke, I could hear, drifting from the communal room in waves of cadenced strains, the otherworldly harmonies of Mussorgsky's *Night on Bald Mountain.* I closed my eyes. Childhood memories of Disney's *Fantasia* glided past me like falling leaves swept by an autumn gust. The Angelus bell rang in the distance. The first rays of dawn drove vixens and warlocks back to their dens and the gauzy spirits of the dead floated back to their graves for yet another day of rest.

Flight from Ein Sof

TEN

I returned to the gloomy depths of Gehenna looking for answers. I'd been perusing Spinoza's *Ethics* and Einstein's Theory of Special Relativity. Separated by three centuries, the philosopher and the physicist had both studied relativity, the first to explore the metaphysical realm, the second to postulate immutable cosmic laws. They reached broadly similar conclusions, among them that perception depends on vantage point.

Spinoza buoyed his argument by proposing -- swiftly earning him excommunication and centuries of Jewish and Christian antipathy -- that much of human consciousness is based, not on fact, but on how we are conditioned to interpret the occurrence of *being*. There are no wrong answers, he proposes, only divergent opinions which are themselves blurred by conformity to an acquired optic. In other words, truth is in the mind's eye of the beholder.

Einstein also theorized that reality is merely an illusion, *"albeit a very persistent one."* He went a step further. He declared that perceptions can actually alter the experience of reality. I had an opportunity to test this strange concept, not in the perfect geometry of space, nor in the sterile labyrinths of Cartesian logic, but in a realm that has grown and spilled over its own boundaries like a gangrenous sore, far from the synthetic harmony of Ein Sof where the well-to-do live in stifling isolation.

It was still dark as I worked my way to the bridge. I came upon sleepy-eyed children pulling heavy loads, sweaty cadaverous men packed like sardines in rickety trucks belching black smoke, half submerged under the garbage they were ferrying from one end of the chasm to the other. *Perpetual* garbage, I reckoned.

Huddled like newborn pups against the scurfy wall of an abandoned building, young boys slept, their arms crossed against the chill of night, their fingers clasping their shoulders. Others, stirring from a thin, turbulent slumber, were getting ready, in lieu of breakfast, to take the long and excruciating way out of reality by sniffing glue.

Further on, resting on a bed of filthy rags near the gutter, a woman dozed fitfully with an infant at her breast while an older child begged for scraps of food and wiped an ever-runny nose on the sleeve of a threadbare sweater. Ahead, past the bridge, in a huge crater-like depression teeming with vultures, I found toddlers and young teens feeding on garbage. Knee-deep in steaming mountains of waste and competing with the loathsome winged scavengers, another group of youngsters rummaged for a meal, a slipper, perhaps a broken toy to brighten an otherwise joyless childhood.

And when I ventured past the festering hollow, I chanced upon a living ghost. I have no other words to describe her. She has no name. Madness robs people of all identity. Madness, in her case, further sharpens the alienation, the anonymity. She has no name. She has earned the scorn of her own wretched kind and she will pass in this dimension and from this moment in time unnoticed, even by her fellow Dybbuks. Surely, a name, a common moniker would give her substance, if not legitimacy. But she's been forgotten. Insanity and amnesia have mercifully yanked her from the clutches of reality. Yet she is real, irritatingly so, the symbol and victim of the dysfunctional society that spawned her. Shunned, loathed, she inspires revulsion, not mercy, for she is unrepentant, defiant in her grotesque cardboard palace, amid the debris, the scraps of metal, the offal on which she feeds, the useless memories that haunt her still, come rain or come shine, come hell or high water.

Her partner-in-grime, ageless, toothless, feral and mad, too mad to erect her own shelter, sits by her companion's side or steals forty winks on the naked pavement, curled up in a fetal position, her two hands pressed together to form a cushion under her cheek. Wielding a yard of rubber tubing, or an old broom, she chases after man and specter with equal fury, a menacing fist raised against oncoming traffic and snickering children, striking the ground with anger and bewilderment, no, with exasperation, spitting at passers by, pelting them with invectives. Sometimes folly crests like an open flame and a torrent of tears drenches her grand-motherly face. Overwhelmed by the sheer intensity of her frustration, she calms down, tunes in briefly on the world around her, then resumes her silent vigil, a lifeless gaze now focused on an all-consuming void.

One day, a gang of thugs swooped down on Gehenna and smashed the paper, string and plastic scaffolding her friend had erected. Even a place of torment such as Gehenna, I mused, has its pitiless enforcers, its dim-witted disciplinarians. The woman put up a fierce battle but the enforcers prevailed. Trampled by uncaring feet, the decimated remains of her flimsy abode were carted away and thrust aside under the bridge where Ein Sof's trash and raw sewage eventually end up. She was allowed to bed down on the bare ground and fend for herself.

Up the road, in the narrow, slop-splattered alley that hugs the flanks of an old church, a man writhed in drug-induced agony. Frothing at the mouth, his eyes on fire, he crumbled to the ground and let out a blood-curdling wail. Clawing at the demons that tormented him, thrashing about, he rolled into the gutter and narrowly missed being hit by a speeding garbage truck.

Safe in their pews, the faithful were being treated to the grand spectacle of a pre-dawn mass. "*Dominus vobiscum,*" said the priest. "*Et cum spiritu tuo*," the faithful responded, mercifully unmindful, if only for a brief moment in their beleaguered lives, of the pervading godlessness that surrounds them.

Around the corner, propped against a fence, a group of cripples flaunted their grotesque infirmities. Unruffled, passers-by, the faithful, the penitent, the aimless and the lost, the discarded and the redundant, stepped over them like so much rubbish. Across the street, a young woman sprawled on the ground breast-fed her newborn as three older daughters, sired by three different men, plied the beggar's trade.

Who are the mad, I reflected, and who are the meek who inherit the wind? As I pondered the question, I nearly tripped on the cadavers of several children. They lay prone, splotches of dried blood streaking their faces. They'd been bound and gagged and shot, gangland-style, in the back of the head. Even Gehenna has its pariahs.

The only thing that separates "God" and its creation is a dissimilar perspective. Relativity prevents either from switching places. In Gehenna, as in Ein Sof, where heaven and hell coexist in perilous proximity, right and wrong are less sharply defined. For the powerful, the privileged, the favored, the free, the well fed who squander their freedom by abdicating to the tyranny of orthodoxy, truth remains the stronger of two or more conflicting views. For the poor, the disenfranchised, the forgotten, the unloved, the Dybbuks and the ghouls and the zombies that haunt the conscience of the Perpetuals, the truth is a useless paradox, like relativity. Don't look for answers, I kept telling myself. Don't look for reason. All you'll find is nature, cruel and unmoved, further debased by the aggregate interests and avarice of the dominant power base.

●

It was now nearly dawn but the sun had yet to rise behind Gehenna's battered ramparts. An ashen darkness still clung like a shroud over its higher elevations. Up since the cocks' first crow, Gloria (I gave her that name to memorialize this fleeting apparition) raced down the sheer, narrow footpath leading to the murky waters of the creek below. Pressed to her bosom, swaddled in an old piece of cloth and still asleep, her infant daughter was oblivious to it all. The course is overrun with hazards but Gloria knows every crag, every loose pebble, every muddy ledge along the way. She's made the perilous trek a thousand times or more since the birth of her baby, six months ago, and she negotiates each obstacle with the agility of a veteran climber.

Laden with her precious cargo, a pail of water now balanced atop her head, she turned around and clambered back uphill. Midway, she stopped to catch her breath. She must manage her strength. She's pregnant with her second child and she's hardly eaten in the past three days. But Gloria is no stranger to privation. Pain no longer daunts her. She has her baby to care for. Another little one is on the way in five months or less, she's not sure.

Slowly, night's inky mantle dissolved, baring a pale orange sky. A new day had dawned, bringing a fresh surge of anticipation and energy. Emboldened, she resumed her arduous climb.

Gloria is fourteen.

Reaching the summit, winded by the grueling ascent, Gloria wiped her brow and surveyed her surroundings. Before her, barely visible in morning's timid glow, stretched, familiar and inescapable, an unobstructed view of utter barrenness, of squalor and malignancy and evil that the thick haze failed to conceal. Behind her, balancing precariously on the edge of a narrow bluff overgrown with stinkweed, rests the ramshackle hut Gloria calls home. Straddling a scaffolding of rotting wood pylons and corroded iron beams under which cower a small emaciated dog and a palsied cat, the windowless shack stands defiant in its vulnerability, a symbol of the paradox that is Gehenna.

Gloria blows out the quivering flame of an old kerosene lamp and fans away the acrid emanations. She lays the sleeping infant on the floor, gently propping her head against a cardboard box where she keeps all of her possessions. There's a rag doll, an old discolored dress, a small bundle of used baby clothes, an old photograph, a broken comb, a tin of cereal, a jar of brown sugar in which tiny yellow ants have taken residence, a cross fashioned from popsicle sticks, a faded prayer book frontispiece in which an enraptured blue-eyed blond Jesus is seen levitating above a sea of mesmerized disciples.

Gloria strikes a match, ignites kindling in the hollow of a cinder block and stirs a thin gruel of rice and water into a pitted metal bowl. She stopped breast-feeding her daughter when she became pregnant with her second child. Underweight, her ashen skin pocked with mosquito bites, the baby girl suffers from malnutrition. Gloria looks at her daughter with a mixture of tenderness and apprehension as her own childhood, barely tasted, irretrievably lost, comes back to haunt her.

Gloria is the embodiment of innocence undone, childhood compromised and corrupted by poverty, neglect and hopelessness. Soft-spoken and unassuming, she reluctantly relives the nightmare by evoking it at my urging. Her narration, despite the horror it inspires, is childlike and flat. Her voice betrays neither anger nor sorrow. She smiles timidly instead, perhaps to hide the shame and pity she feels, not for herself, but for those who so sadistically deprived her of love and dignity.

I asked her what she desired most and felt instantly shamed by the vacuity of my question. Fixing a gaze of unfathomable emptiness at some distant point in space, giving me time to ponder my lack of tact, then turning tenderly to the toddler nestled in her arms and patting her own belly, the child-mother replied, "I have nothing and I have everything. I can't ask for less or for more."

In the world of Dybbuks, nothing and everything are usually too much to bear.

Morning alit, or something akin to morning. A faint gray glow crept out of an overcast horizon. The glow was not bright enough to disperse the misty tendrils of fog that hung like wispy ghosts over the desolation.

•

Gehenna, like fungus, has spread tentacle-like, sprouting squalid slums along muddy ridges and down the slopes of dank garbage-strewn ravines.

It's in one such slum, nicknamed Limón by the locals because of the jade-green stream of sludge that runs through it, that I came across Angela. I found her sitting at the edge of a cot, her feet pitted by insect bites and glistening skin lesions, in a shed under a leaking corrugated sheet metal roof held up by rotting wooden beams.

In a corner of the room, under the pallid rays of a bare 40-watt bulb around which a squadron of flies and moths kept circling, propped on a table littered with rags and old newspapers, rested a tall, garishly painted plaster figurine, a Madonna and child whose introspective, tortured gaze, frozen skyward where God is said to dwell, exuded pain and disillusionment, betrayal and stupefaction. Every once in a while, almost mechanically, the girl cast a forlorn glance at the holy icon, perhaps for reassurance. But in her large brown eyes all I saw were false hopes and broken promises.

This time I said nothing. Assailed by a jumble of emotions, I just looked at her cherub face. I wanted to hug her and, in so doing, to absorb her within my being for warmth and reassurance. But I didn't dare. I took her little hand in mine and kissed it. Angela blushed, looked at the bare concrete floor and sighed.

"Take her away from this place," her mother pleaded.

Take her? Where? How? What do I know about the transmigration of souls? When was the last time I rescued anyone from a nightmare? What if this was a trap? What if *this* Dybbuk was an incubus, an evil spirit? I understood what sophistry can do to distort judgment, to cripple reason, to inspire fear, to justify cynicism. And as I looked at Angela's innocent face, I chose discretion instead of valor. I ran out and burst into tears.

Outside, the vultures, the ever-present vultures, resumed their abominable vigil, gliding overhead like black-winged demons at a Witches' Sabbath, awaiting death, smelling it, almost tasting it. Surely I reflect, even God must find Limón a very bitter fruit.

Flight from Ein Sof

ELEVEN

"Fabian is a weakling, a coward. He was a miserable, weepy child who shunned responsibilities, recoiled from physical exertion and took pleasure at fomenting intrigues that deepened the chasm separating me and his mother. Tears came easily to him, the way they do to an actor or a charlatan."

That's how Abraham described his son to me during a hastily convened secret meeting. Abraham had slipped a note in my pocket when no one looked.

"Please come to my room at noon. You must know what I know."

Careful not to arouse suspicion, eager to know what Abraham knew, I left the communal lunch table on some pretext and made my way to my great-great-grandfather's room.

"We don't have much time," he said. "I can't keep this secret any longer. It's consuming me, poisoning my days, haunting my nights. Please hear me out.

"Legends sprout new limbs with every retelling but lies never die. They grow stronger and more difficult to refute. Fabian mastered the art of pretense long before his mother passed away, and he exercised it with malicious skill well after I remarried. Truth be told, my first wife was a shrew, a coarse and irritable woman who punished me for much of our marriage because I didn't match the grotesque blueprint of the perfect husband that existed only in her mind. I took it on the chin for as long as I could. I said nothing to kin or relations. I didn't even confide in my rabbi. Only Fabian knew the inner turmoil that consumed me, only he heard the shouting matches, the ugly words, only he witnessed my sleepless nights, my moments of despair so profound, so devastating that I often contemplated suicide."

Abraham paused, besieged by memories, overwhelmed by the weight of words rehearsed but never spoken.

"The boy was incapable of saying a kind word; he never put his arms around me. And he never saw the tears I shed when no one looked."

"But you did engage in an extra-marital affair, didn't you," I ventured with staggering hypocrisy. "Surely that was bound to envenom your life."

"Yes, I began to see another woman, young, vibrant, attentive, loving, and in her arms I recaptured my own waning youth and discovered that I possessed undiminished reserves of love that needed to be shared. When Fabian's mother died, I married her. I was the happiest man on earth. All the years of conflict and turmoil dissolved in one magnificent, cathartic, rejuvenating burst of euphoria. Instead of sharing my joy, Fabian proceeded to spoil it for us from the start. He criticized her cooking, ridiculed her childlike exuberance, mocked her amorous nature and conspired to destroy our relationship."

"He was jealous. He felt slighted. His mother had died and you now lavished your love and attention on another woman."

"Fabian never really loved his mother. He resented her tyrannical governance and loathed me for cowering like a dog and surrendering to her aberrant whims. I will never forget when, enraged by something his mother had said, he lunged at her, grabbed her by the throat, lifted her off the floor and pinned her against the wall. I thought he was going to kill her. I just stood there, stunned, elation secretly coursing through my being.

"One day, when Fabian caught my new wife and me in a tender moment in the kitchen, he lounged at her, pulling her away from me and screaming, 'You're not my mother! Get away from my father.'"

"What about the attic? He told my father that he was forced to..."

"Repeated often enough, lies take on the appearance of truth. Fact is it was his choice. He could have slept in his own room, under the thick eiderdown we had bought him. But bedding down in the attic reinforced his self-inflicted sense of martyrdom. Besides, in winter, with the wood-burning stove on all night, the attic was the warmest part of the house. And in summer, with the bull's-eye windows ajar, the attic was breezy and cool."

"Fabian also alleged that he was being fed leftovers."

"Nonsense. There was always a setting for him at the table but he refused to eat with us. When hunger finally tugged at his innards, he'd devour the odds and ends we had set aside."

"Is it true you sent him away, miles from home?"

"I had no alternative. He was surly and combative. He made my new wife's life miserable. So I apprenticed him to a friend of mine, a candle maker because he had no disposition for anything else. He was fired twice for laziness and insubordination, and I had to beg my friend to take him back. He grew up, a morose, pugnacious, unmotivated individual who blamed the world for his own shortcomings and sought refuge from imaginary affronts in confrontation or tearful lamentations."

Abraham looked at me, his eyes ablaze, shaking his head as if to say, "Do you get the picture now?" Then he looked down at his feet, sadness turning to shame.

"The apple never falls far from the tree. Fabian's own son, your grandfather, also a candle maker, did not amount to much. Seldom gainfully employed, he had no real trade. He kept a small candle-making business but he was too proud to work. He spent much of his time at the synagogue or immersed in his precious books -- the Torah, the Talmud, the Zohar -- or strolling up and down Main Street, deep in thought and attired in fine three-piece suits bought on credit and rarely paid for.

"So now you know. Not a word to anyone, you hear! Let the others believe what they wish. I'll do without their sympathy as I have all these generations."

I took Abraham's wizened hand into my own and held it for a moment.

"You can count on me."

I then put my arms around him. He wept.

TWELVE

Gehenna. Something keeps pulling me back. Is it what the French call *"le goût de la fange,"* literally "a taste for muck," that sudden and inexplicable craving to forfeit all civility and refinement, to leap headfirst into a pit of filth and depravity where humankind's most repulsive down-and-outers congregate?

Or is it something else, perhaps the urge to gawk at humanity in its most dismal state? The compulsion to touch it and be smeared in the process? Is it morbid pity or gruesome voyeurism? Do I revisit Gehenna to survey it or to cohere? Am I an intruder or the prodigal son reconnecting with his roots? Haven't I seen enough shit and degradation and misery and despair when I ventured into the monster's entrails during my years as a reporter? Having since confessed to a waning passion for humanitarian causes, what repulsive addiction entices me still?

But I keep going back, anticipating the putrefaction and the decadence and the apathy and the endless struggles that crush the outcasts, the unwanted, the unloved. In the bleak and malodorous pit of despair that is Gehenna, when love and hatred are gone, all I stumble on is indifference.

•

My friend, the novelist William Lewis once wrote, *"Children are like stars. They are lost in the flesh of the night; but they can be found because they shine. It is when they become the blackness that we cannot see them, that they cease to be children, that they are lost."*

What I found in the eyes of a boy I chanced upon in Gehenna was blackness, the kind of burning ebony that exuded from my cousin Amos' eyes as he lay dying. His star may be larger than life but its radiance is fading like that of an exhausted supernova. He will not be reborn from its embers.

"Things could be worse," the boy tells me with apocalyptic intensity. "Life could be forever." Such blighted hope is inexplicable in someone so young. His cynicism is finely tuned, deeply felt. He has seen the dark side, endured the vulgarity of survival, faced the demons.

He's 12.

By day the boy's world is the carbon copy of a hundred Gehennas chanced upon in my endless peregrinations: Sweltering heat, a canvas of squalor and misery, teeming masses of world-weary, cynical, tired creatures trapped and swept by some unstoppable momentum. There is an unkempt shoreline and scum-covered canals in which float, half-submerged, the cadavers of apathy -- trash, human waste, broken-down appliances. Grubby side streets are lined with sleazy bars where locals sip warm beer and engage garishly painted harlots, darkened pool halls where drug deals are made, and fast-sex bordellos.

Gehenna continues to spread, fatigued and imperiled, without a plan, without a vision, compromised by the elements, ravaged by age, neglect, apathy. Buildings are cracked, teetering on the brink of collapse. A few eventually crumble in heaps of worn brick and mortar, raising storms of acrid dust in their final agony.

An incessant stream of Diesel-fueled vehicles emit lung-crunching fumes and produce a dissonance of intolerable pitch that assault the ear, grind nerves. Dodging each other, motorcycles, Lilliputian taxis and overloaded carts pulled by underfed mules jockey for space on crowded, unregulated thoroughfares. The frenetic pace only heightens the feeling of weariness and adds to the exhaustion that such momentum creates. It's a place driven by reflex, surviving on hidden reserves of energy akin to frenzy -- or exasperation.

It's also a place that begs to be forgiven, for some of its people have endearing traits; but it also elicits impatience and revulsion. Small squares where young lovers meet to steal kisses are littered. Benches are encrusted with generations of baked-in guano. Loitering aimlessly, spitting dejectedly, old men wait for the passage of time, as if time were a destination instead of a conveyance. A pervasive smell of decay, excrement and death wafts on the wings of intermittent breezes.

At night, after the sun's copper disk has set the sea on fire, Gehenna turns into a den of depravity of Gomorrhan dimensions. No lust, however vile, remains unquenched for very long. Here, demand feeds supply. Human flesh is the commodity of choice, and purveyors abound.

The boy knows all that. Deserted by his parents when he was six, addicted to Resistol, he succumbed to the vile commerce, to survive, to cheat reality. There is no shame and degradation when hunger beckons and hopelessness warps all reason. But he is paying the ultimate price for clinging so passionately to life. He is dying of AIDS, the same ravenous, diabolical scourge that claimed my cousin Amos.

Illiteracy, poverty, alcoholism, irresponsible paternity are all at work in Gehenna. Some families have not a gram of conscience when it comes to procreation. Use of Resistol among the kids is widespread. It's sold freely everywhere. Pimps and sex tourists often pay the children with cans of the deadly shoe glue. It's a case of turpitude further debased by criminal negligence.

In the hovel where he is cared for, the boy drifts between excruciating awareness and merciful stupor. Eternal night draws near. He will soon be free. Outside, mumbling incoherently, a madwoman, bedraggled, froth caking the corners of her mouth, exchanges stones and insults with vagrants who taunt her. Hoping to squeeze the last traces of pity from a parade of self-absorbed passers-by, an armless, legless man wriggles his way toward some unknown destination like a grub on a sizzling sidewalk. Crying with studied constancy and resonance, a beggar exposes a newborn at her naked left breast.

Feral dogs, traumatized by hunger, rejection and loneliness, respond to a friendly whistle or the offer of a caress with sidelong glances filled with sadness, mistrust, fear. Head low, tail tucked between their legs, panting, they have surrendered to forces heretofore unimagined, now braved with stoic resignation. They do not have the energy to bark.

In the distance, standing legs wide apart for maximum balance in the shade of a big old tree, a policeman stares catatonically in the void to stay cool, conserve energy, perhaps to guard against the incongruity that surrounds him.

On the street corner, near the Ashmodai Hotel where I spent the night, a man beckons. "Anything you want, man: Dope? Girls? Young kids? Name your pleasure."

I describe him to the policeman but the officer, dressed like a Gilbert and Sullivan admiral, stares at me blankly, his eyes-half shut. He waves me off as if he were shooing away a fly. It's nearly lunch-time. In the noonday heat even duty takes a siesta.

THIRTEEN

The dreaded day had arrived. A week had passed and I had given nary a thought to Yossi's deadline, less yet to the consequences of my decision, which I had made without wavering when he first called on me to enshrine a mindless convention. It's not that I begrudged the custom or questioned its origins or doubted the sincerity of those who lived by it. I didn't really give a damn. What I resented was the high-handed assertion that, owing an accident in pedigree, I was somehow duty-bound to serve as a vehicle for its perpetuation.

"Have you reached a decision?" Yossi asked in his best bureaucratic timbre. All eyes were on me, glowing like cold, implacable searchlights of anticipation.

"I have."

"Well?"

"Well, my answer is no. It's a non-negotiable issue. I'm sorry. I'm not big on tradition. Never was. Tradition has a way of trapping people into a never-ending cycle of reflex behavior that may have a numbing effect on the drudgery of life but does nothing to relieve it. In attempting to homogenize human conduct, tradition also has the regrettable habit of ignoring, nay, of writing off, the individual. Man's happiness and freedom depend on his ability to dominate his environment -- or to escape from it when it suffocates him."

"Only God is free. Man is not," someone shouted from the back of the room.

"How convenient. Look, I'm in no mood to argue. Please find someone else or wait until providence delivers a fresh recruit. I may have a tribal link to the clan but I share none of its principles or convictions. No offense intended."

"Tradition is like a ring," Yossi offered with didactic pomposity. "It is complete within itself, all-encompassing, self-defining, unbroken. It embodies the totality of a people's selfhood, it..."

"I don't wish to be regarded as a member of a group I didn't join."

"But you did. Are you forgetting your heredity?"

"I'm the victim of circumstances beyond my control."

Yossi snarled.

My father smiled. He understood, appreciated satire. He recognized in the firmness of my stance the synthesis of his principles and the manifestation of his teachings.

"Traditions set people apart," I said. "Zealots forget that there are other 'rings' and that those who wear them may have a different understanding of selfhood, not to mention, uh, the restrictive nature of circumference."

"Traditions must be nurtured so that they remain whole, undiluted," Yossi hollered, "so they foster unity, provide inspiration, ensure tranquility."

"I can only wear one ring at a time."

"What about the inspirational and conciliatory nature of tradition? What about the serenity it imparts on those who embrace it body and soul? What about its capacity to spread harmony and peace?"

"Spread peace, you say? Are you naïve or blind? Do you really believe that maintaining a tradition prevents even family members from bickering, from showing off their monumental capacity for tribal rancor and discord?"

Yossi blinked. "What do you mean?"

●

I was all too happy to oblige, to savor, in advance, the unease my words would produce.

Lazar and Yanosh had had yet another heated discussion the other night. They always seem to be at each other's throats. Each begrudges the other's opinions with a passion only clashing egos, not scholarship or reason, can inflame. Their quarrels are petty, volcanic and generally brief but apt to re-ignite at the slightest provocation. The two have turned ideological ranting into a form of dialectic perpetual motion. Round and round they go, holding on for dear life to their cherished positions but, predictably, getting nowhere.

"Surely, friendly disagreements are bound to arise in a close-knit community," Yossi intervened.

True. But instead of letting go or striving for a middle ground, their tempestuous squabble, with "left" versus "right," not fact versus opinion at the center of their quarrel, nearly ended in a fistfight. I had offered to referee and enlisted Néné Jan and Uncle Johnny as alternate arbiters. Yanosh and Lazar agreed, secretly hoping that three mediators would deliver contrasting verdicts resulting in a "draw," thus allowing the antagonists to adhere to their respective positions and declare victory. Closed minds are not interested in right or wrong. All they seek is support for their views and beliefs. Lazar and Yanosh are the type of men who cling to their opinions -- reality be damned.

"So, Lazar," asked Néné Jan, "what is this all about?" Lazar obliged, sounding off with more vehemence than common sense.

"Well," Néné Jan offered cautiously, "I think you may have a point."

"Just a doggone minute," Yanosh fumed. "Why don't you hear me out before surrendering to Lazar?"

"You're right," said Néné Jan. "By all means, proceed."

Pontificating, as is his style, Yanosh told his side of the story.

"You know what," said Néné Jan, "on second thought, I think Yanosh may be on to something."

"Hold it," I intervened. "How can both Yanosh and Lazar be right?"

Uncle Johnny, who had listened quietly, placed a conciliatory hand on my shoulder, looked me in the eye and proclaimed, as if delivering a pithy court summation:

"Tell you what, you're right *too*."

I was baffled but said nothing. I felt that Uncle Johnny had let me and the two rivals down, that his ambivalent verdict was a monument of vacillation and frivolity. Anxious to make peace, he did the truth a disservice. Or so I thought. I was wrong. As I reviewed the doctrinal differences that so diametrically and pointlessly divide Lazar and Yanosh, I also pondered my uncle's Solomonic ruling. Drawing from Zen, to which I turn when western dogmatism gets in the way, I suddenly apprehended Johnny's awesome and disarming wisdom. I then examined my own "convictions," and found them to be less than firm or unfailing. Depending on the issues, I allow them to oscillate from pole to pole. Those who seek the truth, I keep telling myself, are infinitely closer to it than those who claim to have found it. In so doing, I grant myself the right to change my mind as often as it takes to find it.

Sometimes, the only way to understand and acknowledge the scope of a problem is to confront it with an open mind. This is something that Yanosh and Lazar doggedly refuse to do. They'd rather cling to their convictions than risk being proven wrong. They stopped searching. They've wrapped themselves in the security blanket of fixed ideas, shut the door tight against the very light of knowledge, and they won't let anyone pry it open. Néné Jan is open-minded and generous but he dithers. Only Johnny, with years of legal experience behind him, makes the connection between apparent truth and incontrovertible fact.

Right like wrong, is what the self perceives. What we see is seldom shaped by irrefutable reality or truth but by conditioning. Often, what we choose to believe is born from an unwillingness to go beyond the obvious. Inflexible ideas are the offspring of intellectual sloth. Yet it seems as if everything is still defined more by form than substance -- radicalism vs. conformity, pious traditionalism vs. dissolute nonconformity. Time has come to shake off absurd labels in describing people's proclivities. Instead, we need to acknowledge our humanity and our ambivalence. The brain is composed of two hemispheres: the right and the left. We also possess a vestigial reptilian brain that often takes over and is apt to subvert reason. In order to attain anything approaching enlightenment, one must first forsake the dualities of "me" and "them," "conservative" and "liberal," interior and exterior, small and large, good and bad, delusion and fact, life and death, being and nothingness.

What others have come to grasp intuitively can never become ours unless we come to understand it through our own mental efforts. Each of us has a different way of reaching the same destination. There isn't just one road and not everyone is fit to travel the same course. By limiting our journey to a single trail, we may be leading ourselves astray.

●

"I fail to see what an insignificant family dispute has to do with anything," Yossi exclaimed.

"Next thing you'll tell me is that wrangling senselessly to protect an opinion is also a family tradition that deserves protection."

"Mock us all you want. You think you're better than us because you can read and write and have traveled the world. Wasn't it the Rebbe Herschel the Pious of Vilnius who called heretics *'those who pride themselves in their superiority to conventional views,'*" Yossi snapped.

"Not exactly. It was 'the eccentric prince of paradox,' the notorious Jew-hater, the Catholic apologist, G.K. Chesterton. And he was wrong. Heretics are freethinking people who question accepted doctrine and faith-based 'truths,' and have the courage to examine the validity of their own beliefs and, if need be, to reject them. They do not go around peddling borrowed superficialities. Pelagius, the 6th century thinker was not a heretic. He believed in the original innocence of man. He did not buy into the ignoble "original sin" concept which asserts that a newborn who dies unbaptized will go straight to hell. He said, 'Who can be so impious as to deny an infant of any age, the common redemption of the human race?' Galileo was not a heretic but a man who saw a truth that contradicted conventional wisdom. Giordano Bruno was not a heretic. He died an early martyr for rationalism and modern scientific ideas. Peruse the long list of 'heretics,' ancient and modern, and you will find an inventory of the greatest minds that ever lived. Ignorance, of which idle knowledge is the most egregious aspect, is the root cause of friction among men. We should all be more interested in truth than in conditional peacemaking."

"Your attitude saddens and offends us. The council of elders will deliberate and decide your fate: Silence or banishment. May the Heavenly Father have mercy on your soul."

"The world has no need of a "heavenly" father. We are cosmic orphans. We need real flesh and blood parents to teach us how to defend ourselves against the tyranny of rigid ideas."

I sought my father's eyes and nodded at him with gratitude. I saw pride in his eyes. My mother turned to him and whispered what I had learned to read on her lips, "Look at the son I gave you." My father, conceding with humility that his role in my procreation had been negligible, nodded at her in return with a smile.

The others looked at me with scorn. All but Lucy, who had shit in her bloomers and been rushed to the bathroom, and Tante Yetta, who had dozed off in anticipation of a sonnet by her beloved Néné Jan. Yanosh scrubbed his hands with renewed vehemence. My grandfather buffed his chrome-plated pistol, bringing it up to his face to see if the silvery sheen of the barrel reflected his likeness.

Helen was furiously pounding plums into a pulp in her big copper vat. Rocking back and forth in her chair, lost in a self-induced trance, Meema fought her demons with incoherent incantations peppered with threats and Judgment Day curses. Lazar talked to his kitten. Néné Buby and Tante Fanny were deep into a game of mah-jongg. My grandmother, who hadn't bothered to follow the proceedings, was deep into an early chapter of *A Tale From Bali*, by Vicki Baum. In the dark eyes of my cousin Amos, pretty and graceful as a girl when he was a mere child, I saw the inconsolable grief of a man, now passed his prime, who paid a high price for his love of lithe, muscular, sexually well endowed young men. Looking for attention, Fabian drowned in a deluge of tears that ceased when my aunt Mary, still cradling her dolls, offered him kind words. Abraham, for the first time since we had met, smiled at me openly and with manifest tenderness.

Flight from Ein Sof

FOURTEEN

"The council of elders met yesterday evening. We deliberated late into the night. With several votes for, several against and four abstentions, we decided to offer you one last chance to reconsider and accept the post of clan leader which, upon completion, will earn you a seat in the council and full voting privileges. What do you say?"

"My esteemed uncle, I stand before you, helpless, castrated by your intransigence. What choices are you offering me? Either I submit to your will or I suffer the consequences. There is no middle ground. We cannot barter, haggle, negotiate, compromise. It's your way or no way, isn't it?"

"You don't understand," said Yossi in a tone simulating affability.

"Oh, I understand far more than you give me credit for. But since we're on the subject of misreading or misjudging -- another ploy to exploit the last vestiges of hesitancy that I may still harbor -- let me entertain you for the last time with an incident none of you has yet had the pleasure to lament. And let's see if *you* find it instructive enough to relent and let me be. O.K.?"

Yossi shrugged. Néné Buby gobbled like a turkey and blinked several times, overcome by a sudden fit of Tourette's. Meema, scowling, waved an impatient hand.

"Pfft! This boy's always been full of tall tales. Do we have to listen to yet another one of his grotesque yarns?"

Someone in the back of the room, my grandmother, I think, intervened.

"Damn right, let him speak."

Yossi arched his eyebrows and sighed. "Go ahead if you must."

•

Must? Hell, I "*must*" nothing. I knew I was wasting my time, squandering my mental energy. Yossi and his flunkies see things their own way. Rituals, traditions, ceremonials, however absurd they seem to an uninvolved observer are as vital to them as is the "*smell of napalm in the morning*" to a flag-waving lieutenant-colonel who gets his jollies sauntering through a hail of exploding mortar shells. It's the manna that sustains them. I shouldn't have to justify myself. These people speak an alien dialect and our brains are wired differently. It takes a leap of logic and extraordinary courage to reject customs that were drummed into us since childhood; and some people simply can't or won't part with them. They're not really interested in pursuing a dialogue in which give-and-take and fair play lead to rational discourse and, perhaps, a meeting of the minds. All they want is to mulishly follow the stream of a conversation they are having in their own head to its ultimate doctrinaire conclusion.

•

"In open societies," I began, drawing from a store of memories, "freedom of conscience and an independent press are both an asset and a guarantor of democracy. In other parts of the world, an outspoken press is viewed as a threat to oligarchies and other deeply entrenched power structures. This attitude creates a self-view by the press that predisposes it to timidity and, often, to inaction. Publishers, indebted to their advertisers and sponsors for their precious revenues, are loath to antagonize them. Journalists, afraid they might lose their job or their neck, probe less deeply than they should. Empowered by the elite, beholden to them, governments add insult to injury either by pretending not to know or by sacrificing the messenger. I've always believed and publicly stated that a nation that controls or restrains its media, or fosters a climate of fear and intimidation that cows it into self-censorship -- or silence -- is a nation of thugs."

"Yes, so?"

"So I said so again, loudly and clearly not long ago, following a drive-by gangland-style massacre that claimed five lives and scorched the soul of a quaint and skittish Central American village habituated to intermittent violence and accustomed to looking the other way.

"Five people. Was it an accident? Was it vengeance? Were they victims of mistaken identity? Were they felled in a drunken rapture, as one report alleged, by giddy fans celebrating a soccer victory? Or were they targeted for assassination in a drug deal gone awry? Speculation was rife. When the smoke lifted, dozens of spent AK-47, 40mm- and 9mm-caliber shells lay on the ground, silent accessories in a drama that began and ended with lightning speed in the rain after dusk. The spent shells offered few clues. Everyone is armed in these parts and firing weapons in the air to ring in the New Year, make merry, cheer a wedding party, exult the birth of a male heir or just blow off steam is as sacred a ritual as kissing and drenching with tears the feet of the local patron saint whose garishly painted effigy, carved in wood, is paraded during the annual all-Saints procession."

"Where is this leading to?"

"I'll tell you. There's nothing like a community that hurriedly mops up the blood, plugs up the bullet-riddled walls with cement and seals its collective lips in a terror-driven reflex to sharpen fear and blunt one's sense of well-being. Nothing like a craven and dimwitted constabulary (the murderers got away and the leads grew cold) to cast grave doubt on the probity of the local cops and resurrect rumors of criminal collusion. Nothing like a timid, controlled press (one paper buried the story on page 56; another on page 75; when contacted, the other two mainstream rags declined to talk about the case) to reflect on a society's health and moral fiber. Nothing like yet another senseless crime in a region long overwhelmed by lawlessness, traumatized by the greed, arrogance and ineptitude of successive regimes, and disgraced by the ceaseless suffering of its people, to explain that peace and prosperity are but a distant dream."

I hear the sound of wearied behinds fidgeting in their seats.

"When it comes to bad news, the villagers react with robotic conformity. Keeping quiet being the simplest form of disinformation, they say nothing or change the subject. If pressed, they deny and abjure events that still give them nightmares. It's gossip in reverse. Endowed with a capacity for infinite permutations, this denial-by-explication of indisputable facts is a skillfully knitted filigree of extenuation, distortions and absurd rationalizations, all artfully commingled and interlaced to befuddle the curious or the inquisitive."

Meema sighs with impatience.

"When persistent probing and insightful conjecture meet with stony silence, when doors slam shut, when friendly smiles turn to scowl, the truth, gruesome and rank, is surely lurking underfoot like a viper squeezing beneath a rock. Asking too many questions in a hamlet that pulls in its sidewalks at dusk is as perilous an endeavor as it is brazen. Attempts to shed light on an unsolved earlier murder drove this point home and forced me to make a hasty retreat back home not so very long ago. Efforts to get to the bottom of the most recent carnage were similarly thwarted.

"I said all that in a widely published commentary. I added that silence invites more brazen acts of violence, more deaths. I cautioned that, armed merely with words, journalists wage an ill-balanced war. The other side has inflexible beliefs. Or guns.

"I concluded by warning that while growing discontent over the degradation of life -- poverty, inflation, violence, human rights abuses and political apathy -- is the leading cause of unrest, a muzzled society and a cowardly press are apt to bring a country to the brink of civil disorder.

"I said much more but I don't want to bore you. Make a long story short, my night behind bars for 'casting aspersions on the town, vilifying the local constabulary and defaming the nation's character,' was instructive. As I sat on a cold, rough-hewn stone bench, inspecting the damp, graffiti-etched walls on which scurried gigantic cockroaches and hideous spiders, and gauging the strength of the massive iron door, I realized that while my body was being held captive, presumably to cleanse my slanderous soul, I didn't for a moment feel confined. Yes, there were thick partitions between me and my fellow inmates, high battlements separating me from the multitudes of faceless people sleeping the sleep of the righteous in their own beds. And yet there was between me and my custodians a vast and impenetrable rampart they could not breech -- my freedom to think, my right to say things people don't want to hear. If my jailers had silenced me for good, as they are wont to do in these parts with consummate skill and relish, I would pass on knowing that while idealists can be gagged, once spawned their ideas take a life of their own and, like matter, cannot be destroyed.

"Predictably, I was released the next morning and declared *persona non grata* when the authorities concluded that I was more of a nuisance than a threat. So I ask you now, what am I? A nuisance or a threat?"

My question was met with silence interrupted by a few discreet fits of coughing. Sometimes a cough is the synthesis of eloquence. Or prudence.

•

When a child kneads a lump of clay, what he fashions is a symbol. The result hints at an object that has no real connection to its intended meaning or reality. Traditions, to which people are entitled, but which they have no right to impose on others, are golden calves to me, ideological idols I refuse to regard as instruments of veneration. Tradition adjusts itself to the memory of what those icons represent and which, because they evoke some primeval and atavistic but blurry memory, can only be sustained through the reiteration, from generation to generation, of self-perpetuating legends and rituals.

●

"A nuisance? That's an understatement," Meema yelped. "A nuisance *and* a threat. And to think that I once offered him a glass of tea and cookies."

"The tea was watery and the cookies were stale...."

"Never mind all that," Yossi intervened. What are you getting at?"

"What I am getting at is that I was not born to be confined. Not by man nor by his word. I shall breathe at my own pace, as deeply or as faintly as I choose. Your traditions may be benign, including the one you insist I embrace for the common good and tranquility of the clan. My mind is made up. Accepting the leadership of the clan, symbolic and temporary as the post may be, would force me to abjure my own values. Remember, I am the black sheep of the family. You have nothing to gain by forcing your mores on me. I won't be silenced, title or no title. It's for that reason that I decline. Consider it an act of extraordinary charity on my part. The distance between a nuisance and a threat is minute. My decision is final."

"Suit yourself. We will deliberate your fate and get back to you by sundown. Remember: There are no individuals here. You are either part of the community or you are not."

Where had I heard that before?

FIFTEEN

So, what dreadful punishment would the elders prescribe? Would I be merely spurned and reduced to silence, like Abraham? Or would they reserve a harsher ordeal, the kind that only the bruised egos of snubbed missionaries can conjure up?

For a brief instant, spurred by anger, I considered absconding to Gehenna, never to return. Gehenna: an underworld of burning garbage and souls on fire. Raw. Inclement. Dangerous. Down-to-earth in its uncompromising complexity, in the dreariness of its relentless reality. Cruel and pitiable. Loathsome and heartbreaking. Vile and tragic. Everything about Gehenna takes me back to the primeval horrors I had chronicled a lifetime earlier, and which my impassioned reports, the millions in foreign aid, the perseverance of private organizations and the dedication and generosity of armies of volunteers had failed to eradicate.

Words survive in the impersonal, two-dimensional realm of the printed page, but they fail to bring change. Instead, they leave a wasteland of lofty rhetoric, sublime yearnings and exalted covenants that do nothing to alter human nature, chill passions, curb hatred. Some horrors are simply too shocking for words or, as deconstructionist philosophy suggests, writing is a dangerous substitute for living as it is likely to sacrifice fact in favor of personal perception.

•

Ebbing passion and waning romanticism in the presence of horror produce a different kind of desolation, one felt deeply in an inaccessible region of one's soul. For years I thought that one way of erring on the side of justice was to side unerringly with the victims of injustice -- the vanquished, the dispersed, the humiliated, the persecuted, and the forgotten. Behind prison walls. At mass graves and hurriedly dug sepulchers. Wherever voices of dissent and cries for freedom had been hushed. Amid the anonymous bones scattered about the steaming earth. Pogroms, torture, war, genocide, ethnic cleansing. They'd all become a blur in an unceasing tempest of human agony. In-your-face prime-time images of man's inhumanity to man don't lie. Our world, the evening news reminds us, is a sewer in which we wade, knee-deep, in the blood of martyrs. Gathered around the dinner table, we watch them die or fade away like ghosts. "Past is prelude," we declare with snooty condescension. We owe it to our fragile, overtaxed psyches to forget an endless stream of atrocities -- Shoah, the massacre of native Americans, Biafra, the intertribal carnage between Hutus and Tutsis, the bloodbath in Chiapas and the Guatemalan highlands, Bosnia, the 60-year-old blood-letting between Israelis and Palestinians, Iraq, Afghanistan, the wanton murder of street children.

Distance, racial differences, cultural incongruities, all help intellectualize other people's agony. We endure it by perfunctorily purging our souls after each act of infamy. "You can't change human nature," we pontificate, as we partake of dessert. In a pinch, a mind-numbing sitcom will help set our minds at ease. We survive the truth by looking the other way.

The heavy capital of idealism and exuberance I had invested in unmasking vampires had by now steadily dwindled. The reason for this weariness was not a lack of energy or a diminished commitment to justice, but the cumulative effect of disappointment and disgust at people crippled by indolence and lethargy. I had spent nearly two decades fighting their battles as if they were my own, my activism exhausted in a futile effort to agitate the popular conscience, to stiffen backbones weakened by despotism and exploitation. In so doing, I had finally hit a brick wall and the stars the impact produced in the back of my eyes showered me with an insight of blinding clarity. At long last, I understood that mine was a puny and hopeless contest against formidable foes. I realized that people don't change, seldom rebel, not on the streets, not at the polls. A short memory and a weak character will do that to people. Neither alienation nor profound discontent will spur them to shake the political dustbin. Fearful of change, unnerved by serious reformation, they will choose to be seduced by the echo of old, hackneyed words rather than awakened and aroused by the unsettling resonance of truth.

Passive, submissive, the masses never look back, except to reminisce about a blurry and irretrievable past. They're too busy existing and procreating like lemmings to realize that they're being fleeced, that they're being led to the slaughterhouse then devoured by the very shepherds entrusted with their care. Occasionally, they give in to knee-jerk reactions, a primordial reflex now reduced to feeble tics that are promptly stilled by police truncheons and extrajudicial executions. Feeling the sting of injustice and institutionalized villainy, they will succumb to a brief and atypical act of defiance that horrifies the flock then is promptly swept under the rug of public indifference. Anticipated and tolerated by the oligarchy, these random displays of exasperation are then loudly flouted as the undesirable and expendable byproducts of a free society, instead of being recognized and deplored as the signs of grave social ills.

For lack of a cohesive voice, the souls that haunt all the Gehennas of the cosmos -- apathetic if not inert -- will continue to rely on people who know how to stir their messianic hopes of deliverance from the here-and-now but who spend their time polishing the next speech instead of cleaning up the shit, which is what they were appointed to do in the first place.

Most will be content to live with slogans instead of stirring from the stupor of their political gullibility. Egalitarianism does not work in a vacuum. It requires active participation by all. Its tender shoots will wilt so long as people continue to bask in the feeble light of a fuzzy ideology instead of becoming its mirror. A basic right of democracy, and a key responsibility, is to make leaders accountable for their words, responsible for their broken promises, punishable for their lies. I could stand on the old weather-worn bridge and lecture the people of Gehenna, fanning their resentment, stirring their wilted passions, urging them that long overdue is a paroxysm of nausea, a loud, collective spasm of revulsion at the vampires impaled at their throats. I could convince them that time has come to slam the shutters open and exclaim loud and clear: *"We're mad as hell and we won't take it anymore."* Not the blight and the crumbling sidewalks, not the garbage and the lung-crunching pollution, not the power outages, unregulated traffic, police corruption, influence peddling, drug-running and money laundering, not the gangs and child predators and human traffickers, not the inept and fossilized officialdom, not the Byzantine bureaucracy, lofty promises, limp excuses, words, words, words, not Ein Sof where is mirrored with unbearable realism the lunatic ambivalence of the human spirit.

But such outbursts are dramatized on celluloid in cinemas where the masses purge themselves on Saturday nights or in the bars where the national bile is habitually drowned or on TV where inanity packaged for the hoi polloi turns the brain to mush. At the polls, where the democratic process has been reduced to a thoughtless ritual, there will be no surprises. It will be business as usual. Voters will opt for the "least worst" and hope for the best. That's the safe way out. Convictions are easily subverted by sheepish conformity. In the rush to find whom to blame for their woes, the good people of Gehenna will ultimately exorcise and exonerate their tormentors. There is comfort in *"perpetuity."* It helps deaden hopeless dreams.

SIXTEEN

No. Whatever happens, I will not seek relief from one nightmare by reentering another no matter how much fodder for invective and vilification the experience might provide. My appetite for the offbeat notwithstanding, I would leave Gehenna well alone. Gehenna and its foul, sweltering air, its teeming masses of unwashed bodies, the hideous insects, the gruesome vultures, the green sludge that oozes like the River Styx under a bridge to nowhere, the helpless poor devils who toil without respite from dawn to dusk in an endless and futile transfiguration of birth and death, all the repugnant features of a dysfunctional world I had overlooked as I acted the enforcer in a pit of decadence and filth I mistook for my own exotic playground.

I learned long ago that "exoticism" is a fabrication. It doesn't exist in the real world. It's a myth, a collection of far flung places filled with "quaint and friendly (but inferior) natives," facades manufactured mentally and quickly desecrated physically by misfits and drunks in search of Shangri-La, fragile would-be paradises first sullied by the sword and the cross, by colonialism and proselytism, and later scarred by land speculators and the tourist industry.

Gehenna, like all the palm tree- and hibiscus-fronded archipelagos to which I had retreated in search of Nirvana, was supposed to be foreign and exotic, not recognizable and eerily familiar.

I had fled to increasingly remoter shores, only to find, daubed with different hues, couched in dissimilar tongues and customs, the same stinking quagmire of human misery, superstition, fear, jealousy and obstinacy against the blows of man and nature, of doleful apathy, of absurd hopes and broken dreams, of pain and despair.

I had romanticized the prosaic and the macabre, aware, as I did, that my words, however compelling, and despite the vehemence and passion with which they were voiced, would change nothing.

What happened to the optimism, the zeal, the élan that once inspirited me? Why have disgust, rancor and indifference replaced empathy? Is it age? Is it the realization that I had been screaming at the deaf and gesticulating before the blind and petitioning the dumb and the heartless? Is it the pervading squalor, the immovable structures and rampant corruption in realms so lacking in self-respect, ambition and initiative that they wallow in their own dung and keep faking a smile? Is it the terrifying thought that I had been speaking to myself? Imagine how much time, effort, passion and paper were wasted in the process, how many sounds of anger and pity and disgust and espousal and rejection I had uttered in vain.

●

The elders, the self-righteous poltroons that they are, did not summon me. They rendered their verdict and notified my parents in writing instead. Beaming, tears of joy welling in their eyes, my father and mother took turns hugging me and heaping words of cheer and relief.

"They all voted to expel you from Ein Sof."

"Say that again."

"You're being sent back to Yesod. Isn't that wonderful?"

"What!"

"Yes. Look, it's all here," said my father waving a piece of paper. "They said that anyone who would go to such lengths to defy tradition and jeopardize the social order by challenging it must be mad or desperate. Claiming to be erring on the side of clemency, they settled on 'desperate' but ventured that desperation can lead to madness. They cited 'an intractable incompatibility with the exigencies and rigors of life in Ein Sof' and voted unanimously to send you back to Yesod where your 'anarchism and apostasy are tolerated or better understood.' They added with noticeable sarcasm that entropy -- or a sudden onset of wisdom -- would eventually bring you back you to Ein Sof and deliver you into the bosom of the family."

●

"This means that...." I held my head, fearing it might begin to spin like Linda Blair's in *The Exorcist*. I thought I was losing my mind. "This means that...."

"Yes," my father roared with joy, elated that I had grasped the significance of the elders' verdict.

"So we are destined to go through yet another goodbye," I said, wanderlust and sadness wrestling for control of my battered emotions.

My father waved his hand. "Don't be silly, it's just *au revoir*. Unadorned. Guileless. Down to earth. Low key. Just the way you like it."

"Yes, but...."

My mother smiled and gently placed her hand over my mouth. "There's nothing to say, nothing to do but come to and pick up where you left off. Think of it as a fresh opportunity, the kind of pristine horizon line you've always chased after. No immovable mountains, just the open sea."

"And you two?"

"Our time is up. We belong to your past. We're living on borrowed memories. It has its comical side," my father quipped.

"And the 'clan'?"

"What about it?"

"Why do you put up with all the bullshit?"

My father looked elsewhere.

"You don't understand."

I understood perhaps better than he could ever imagine, with a keenness and sensitivity only empathy and similarity of circumstance can inspire. *Like father, like son.* I had taken shortcuts. Unlike my father, I had defied reason and sidestepped convention, veering away from a course I knew I was not qualified to navigate. Fearing failure, I had circumvented well trodden lanes and cut my own footpaths. I would often boast that I thrived on adventure when, in fact, it was a fear of commitment or a lack of faith in the constancy of my own objectives that catapulted me from one castle-building venture to another. Insufficiently schooled, ill-suited for commerce, undisciplined and ferociously eclectic, I would become what I am less by conscious choice than wishful thinking and naiveté, youthful immodesty and haphazardly self-created opportunities. Necessity, in my case, *was* the mother of invention. My father, a disciplined and scrupulously honest man, had no use for artifice. He conquered his demons far from public scrutiny. Like my mother, he accepted his lot.

"But...."

"Let Abraham explain," my father counseled. He'll do it with far more grace and eloquence than anyone I know. After two centuries of forced silence, he's earned the right to speak for all of us. He will not deceive you."

We hugged, my father, mother and I, and we lingered for a moment clasped in a silent embrace like epiphytes clinging to the tree of life.

"We'll listen to Rachmaninoff and Tchaikovsky," I said to my father as we parted.

"And to Ravel and Debussy and Fauré," said my mother.

"And to Satie and Milhaud and Poulenc," I added. "We'll make it a gala performance.

Flight from Ein Sof

EPILOGUE

I spent my last hour in Ein Sof with Abraham. I had grown fond of the old patriarch. Of all my long departed blood relations, all of whom bore their own heavy cross, it was the despised, the long-suffering Abraham, Abraham the Stoic, Abraham whose voice and dignity had been usurped by lies and stilled by folklore that I understood and in ways not fully apprehended, I identified with.

"There isn't much time, my boy, and so much to tell you. First things first. You're smart, educated and well traveled. But your optic of the world is far too broad to see everything. It misses the details, the minutiae -- you might call them trivialities -- on which average people fixate. Your antipathy for he clan, for what it stands is obvious. But consider this: A clan is a kind of corporate entity. While it's made up of individuals with distinctive person-alities, tastes and proclivities, the clan also has a character, an instinct and a unique life force of its own. It is this essence, primal and unwavering, that compels it to guard against external threats. What Yossi so clumsily tried to put across is that a clan is in peril when any of its members commit, or allow to be committed, acts that could cause it to split up and collapse. In other words, the integrity of the clan can be maintained only by limiting the power and influence of its members."

"But what Yossi expediently ignored," I countered, "what he could never mention without admitting a fundamental flaw in this despotic 'life force' that limits free will, is that the best way to protect a clan is to lead by logic, not zeal, reason, not intolerance. The prophetic order the clan struggles to maintain is at war with freedom of thought. It faces the rest of the world with a mask of unyielding belligerence, feeling threatened in its very being by rational thought whose voice it doggedly tries to silence."

Abraham put his hand on my shoulder. "There is no more free will in the physical world than there is in the world of dreams. The human condition is one of discord. Reason propels us toward higher spheres of being; but the pursuit of hedonism, from which self-perpetuation and the survival instinct derive, slam us back into the most brutish existence. So long as men surrender to the affairs that spring from their transient identity, they imagine themselves to be free. But men are mistaken. They are not free. Men crave structure. We cling to principles the way a man overboard clings to a life raft. Conform, or the gods will be angry. Submit or you will burn in hell. Defiance of the rule of law in the name of justice is no defense, however unjust the law may be."

"Why does everybody give in to such tyranny?"

"For many reasons. Some don't know better. What they see is what they get and it's good enough for them. Others don't dare to speak up. Others yet don't care. So what if their lives are regulated by a symbolic bond, traditions and a few perfunctory rituals? Then there are those who know by intuition or premonition that they have run out of choices."

"Self-deception makes the obvious tolerable."

Abraham smiled. "It's not self-deception. It's deeper than that."

"What do you mean?"

"Human beings have no memory of the future. They exist in the moment, untouched by the passage of time, impervious to the transformations that time sets in motion. They can only relate to their own life experience and they insulate themselves against anticipated depredations by surrendering to reflex. We are all doomed to do what we did before we came to Ein Sof, to engage in the ceaseless repetition of the activities that marked our lives. It makes time pass."

"Or it kills it."

"Suit yourself."

"One last thing, Abraham. What are Dybbuks? Did I imagine them, was I hallucinating or did I really chance upon them in a moment of reckless self-abandon?"

"Dybbuks are human spirits, wandering souls condemned to roam restlessly, burdened by past sins, haunted by pointless dreams. They have always existed. They will never go away. They are our shadows. They are *us* inside out. We don't acknowledge their existence because doing so would force us to confess our own imperfections. You might say we are all Dybbuks-in-training."

"I don't understand."

"You came to us from Yesod -- Hebrew for *foundation*. You're now in Ein Sof. Why do you think they call it that? *Ein Sof* means "no end," infinity, perpetuity. Some even suggest that that Ein Sof is the least offensive definition of an indefinable God. Might as well get used to it. This will one day be your last port of call. You'll submit like the rest of us. You'll learn to subdue your passions."

"Never."

"Never?" Abraham lowered his head and peered at me over his glasses. "Just wait and see. Life is the dream of a future sleep. Waking up puts an end to the hallucination."

"What will I do with all that time, what will I do," I cried out, overcome with a sudden, crushing anguish.

"You'll write, what else. You'll write. I'll dream in the company of Yahweh. And you'll dream in his absence."

He did not elaborate.

●

95

To dream, perchance to be. To be, perchance to cross vast dimensions that transcend psychoanalysis, popular myth and the witless and fraudulent interpretations of the spiritualist fringe. Dreams: winged abstractions that lead dreamers, *thinkers,* to question the validity of conventional canons. Dreams: channels of ideological disobedience. Dreams: the manifestation of folly or the spark that sets off intellectual heresy, whether endured in a lucid state or in the winding and surreal labyrinths that crisscross the psyche. Dreams: Echoes of the bewildering ugliness, cruelty, cupidity, trickery and injustice dreamers witness while awake and stirring. Dreams: a cure against ossified creeds. Dreams: a reminder that freedom is an arm's length away. Dreams: nocturnal musings and daytime reveries that telegraph a host of emotions, buried memories, repressed cravings, a lust for inaccessible pinnacles and a fondness for preposterous hopes. Dreams: an array of uncommon ideas and bizarre perspectives. Crafted in the deepest recesses of the mind, staged against eerie backdrops, spoken in esoteric tongues, dreams challenge reality, defy the status quo and rise against doctrinaire beliefs. Dreaming, for an untold number of people, is an instrument of subliminal rebellion against enforced, often unbearable, reality. Dreams respond to frustration, discontent, anxiety, pain, anger, despair and hope by offering a few milliseconds of cathartic, escapism -- or hours of conscious but uncontrolled contemplation.

Limitless and everlasting, the world of dreams is a realm in which inhibitions and scruples are left at the door. It's the flip side of an actuality vigilantly managed by often dissimilar but tactically congruent interests whose reciprocal objective is to restrain the errant ways of radicals and nonconformists.

•

"What did you just say," I yelled as Abraham floated across the room and merged into the wall.

A disembodied voice responded, "Life is the dream of a future sleep."

"What does that mean," I cried out.

I blinked. Abraham was gone. I looked around me. Several of the people who had come to see me off as I readied to embark for Ein Sof were still gathered around as if frozen in time. The solemn, the sycophants, the snivelers, the kibitzers. They all soon stirred, regaining their voices and momentum like old clocks rewound.

"Go home," I said. "Go home. False alarm. You'll get your chance some other time."

●

Dreams, however lyrical and therapeutic, are no match for reality. Pitiless and cunning, reality always triumphs in the end. It is in defeat that dreamers -- philosophers, poets, musicians, artists, writers and humble workers in the vineyard of negentropy -- find their greatest inspiration. It is in dreams that they seek comfort and hope. To them all I dedicate these musings from the brink where I transited for a time.

Flight from Ein Sof

POSTSCRIPT

I once asked, *"What happens to time when the last clock on earth stops ticking?"* I had tossed the question casually, thinking it whimsical and provocative, a brainteaser worthy of reflection but so thorny as to be ultimately unanswerable. I myself had made no effort to venture into a metaphorical labyrinth from which I might not escape. The question itself was a conundrum, circular and close-circuited and containing within it, I felt, its own enigmatic solution. It was one of those "AHA!" questions; a one-liner a stand-up comic might deliver to daze his audience before firing off other similarly baffling witticisms. And I left it at that.

As my expedition to Ein Sof began to unfold, and for reasons that became obvious when I discovered Gehenna, I wrote an old friend, a scientist, scholar and humanist, asking him if he could work out an answer.

Unruffled, my friend was neither scornful of my riddle nor stumped by it. Instead, he found an existential and ontological component to the question that could be probed and articulated, not in the arcane idiom of mysticism or the dizzying jargon of quantum mechanics but with the clarity of plain talk and with images that reveal the melancholy wit of a contemplative and deeply compassionate man. My friend responded with characteristic punctuality. He wrote:

> *"Clocks are simply a human means of measuring the passage of time. Yet, when the last clock (and I suppose the last human to worry about time) stops functioning, nature will still mark the passage of time. Water will still trickle then gush forward to cut its path and chisel canyons. The sun will shine upon the Earth as it slowly continues a countdown toward its own extinction. Perhaps other creatures will pick up the stress and worry of getting to work on time, eating dinner at the appointed hour, getting to bed and rising (so that they can eventually be wealthy, healthy and wise) -- but these creatures will perhaps have the benefit of four arms so that they are far superior typists.*
>
> *"The universe is composed only of time -- space itself and our filling it with substance and meaning is only an elaborate illusion. Space-time, the creation of early nineteenth century visionaries is, unfortunately, only one more theological stake in the sand that is eventually uprooted by a mile-high glacier that moves a few meters in a decade. Time is a two-dimensional membrane and we, poor creatures, are cast as two dimensional waves of energy upon this surface, which is hurtling past at the speed of light (a process we call the passage of time). We move with this two-dimensional membrane as it expands at the speed of light and this movement provides the illusion of three-dimensional space. Think of a holographic projection on a sheet of paper -- an image that allows us to "see" a three dimensional world within a two-*

dimensional surface.

"As a clock ticks and then comes to rest, the universe experiences nothing gained and nothing lost. There are no means to emerge from time, to stop the world and get off, to separate ourselves from the moment. But when the clock stops ticking, something is forever lost -- both that moment in time and the content of that moment (this loss is what science calls an increase in entropy). The universe loses content and meaning, and burns to a crisp like the very stars around us. Time goes by and the universe does not weep for our passing. Our dust and remains are swept into space, blasted to kingdom come to coalesce with the galactic fireworks and the darkness that surrounds them. Strangely, energy and matter, from which we were created, never disappears, only the means to make them human.

"This year, my mother and father both passed away. I have their remains, a few pounds of dust. Within my mind I see my mother, running and laughing on the beach, forming the glue that once held my personal universe together and filled it with meaning and love. My father's gentle smile has passed from this world. His reassuring glance and his quiet presence is reduced and condensed into a can of ashes mailed to me and now resting on a shelf. When the last clock stops ticking, the world will go on, but the last smile and the last tear shall be gone."

Was my friend echoing Turkish Sufi master, Abdülhamit Cakmut's caveat: *"Everything is meant to serve man. If people are gone from this cycle, nature itself will be over."* Or perhaps, as only a man of science can, did he concede with the cool fatalism of a pragmatist that all knowledge is inaccessible to man and that the bubble of ignorance in which we take refuge harbors us from lunacy and self-destruction?

Spacetime is the fulcrum of modern physics. But what does it really represent? Time seems little more than an allegory, a kind of omnipresent metaphor that permeates all of our earthly experiences. But do our experiences represent a fitting measure of ultimate reality? Perhaps the delusion that we are free *in* time, fools us into believing that we are free *from* time.

The more we probe within ourselves, the more certain we become of the unreality of temporal free will. The only freedom we really possess is the contemplation of untested ideas.